I0772343

THE NAMELESS SHADOW

DARKLING SOULS 1.5

ALEX BREE

ALEX BREE

THE NAMELESS SHADOW

DARKLING SOULS
NOVELLA

CONTENT WARNING

This is a dark fantasy story about monsters with content that may not be suitable for all readers. For a complete content list, please visit the author's website at www.alexbreewrites.com.

THE CONTINENT OF
TERIDAR
Amaryllis
Rexila
Warden's Watch Mts.
The Lost Pass
Avyllon
Brookhaven
Oakwood
Karne
Terre Isthmus
Fangmour
Wildegrove
Heartspring
Wyndsel
Hunger's Teeth Mts.
Warrior's Weald
Sunfyre
Rodarri
Bloodrose Spires
Seven Forests
Titan Cliffs

THE CONTINENT OF
TERIDAR
Amaryllis
Pearl Lake
Rexila
The Golden Road
Avyllon
Brookhaven
Oakwood
Karmo
Fangmour
Wildegrove
Heartspring
Wyndsel
Nyx'ela, Gods'
Tooth Mts.
Warrior's Wealth
Titan Ore Mine
Rodarri
Sunry
Bloodrose Spires
Seven Forests
Titan Cliffs

THE CONTINENT OF

DEMORRA

PROLOGUE

1097 N.T.C. Fifty-five years ago. A small village in the Demorran continent.

Angry smoke coiled in the skies from the flaming village rooftops. His village. Spikes of fear filled the spy's heart as his blood froze. His pack slipped from his shoulders as he took off running, tearing through crushed grass and flying over rocks. Branches whipped him, leaving stinging welts. As the smoke grew nearer, panic overtook him at the thought of what might be burning.

No. No. No.

A wall of heat slammed into him. Homes burned as bleating sheep and goats ran wild through the streets. A man with a ripped shirt stumbled across the road, holding his head as blood poured from a gash. A wailing woman cradled the corpse of her husband, his entrails slipping out. The spy tore through trampled empty gardens, passing a raider's ax stuck in a scorched fence post and a discarded broken sword. Dazed villagers hardly noticed him, and he dared not stop.

Legs and lungs burning, he ran faster—to his own home.

Gods of death and shadows, was Margaret all right? Was his son?

It had to be a raid from one of the wandering tribes. The raiders were long gone, but the destruction remained. And he'd been gone on another mission for the godsdamned tyrant. If only he'd been here... He could've fought. He could've saved them, or at least gotten them out. His boots thundered through debris, and he leapt over rubble.

He raced down the road to his farm. His house was a charred ruin, plunging a knife of terror into his heart. The walls had collapsed, bringing the roof down. It still smoldered, and tendrils of smoke rose into the air. He skidded to a stop before the remnants of his home.

"Margaret! Son!" he called.

No one replied. He flung open the door, forcing himself to ignore the fingernail marks on the inside. Lingering heat spilled from the house, blistering his face. Bleary eyed, he dragged his cloak over his mouth and tore through the timbers. He gripped a fallen piece of the roof and dragged it away. Tendons and muscles in his back were screaming, threatening to snap, but his desperation silenced them. Choking and coughing, he dug his fingers into the ashy side of the wall.

He grunted as the smoldering wood seared his flesh, but he didn't stop. He bellowed and heaved forward, pushing the wall up and up. *Just a little farther. Come on.* The weight threatened to crush him as his legs wobbled from the strain. Pressing his face against the carvings in the wood he'd helped his son make, his heart exploded in fury. He pushed until it tipped backward and revealed the floor of his living room.

His wife slumped beneath a collapsed roof beam. Eyes unblinking, blood trickling from her mouth.

"Margaret!"

Back straining, he freed her from the charred beam. He knelt, cradling her broken body. A bloody dagger fell from her fingers. Her skin was scorched, her lips were black, and her limp body was just starting to grow stiff. She'd been dead for an hour or more. There was nothing he could do.

He stood—he had to find his son. *Gods... please let him be alive.* He roared and attacked the rubble near his wife with his hands, digging in piles of soot and upending the surviving bits of furniture. Nothing.

"Son!"

Skin bleeding and blistering, he shoved his shoulder against the door to their bedroom until it groaned and opened a crack. Digging his fingernails into the wood, he ripped it down. He stepped inside, looking around frantically.

He dug through the smoldering rubble to reveal the hidden cellar door. The safe room he'd prepared for them. His shaky fingertips found the edge of the secret door, and he lifted.

A ball of wet blankets lay inside. He jumped down and unraveled the blankets, praying to every god and goddess.

"Papa?" a small voice said.

Tears forged trails down the soot on his face as he hugged the small, wet form to his chest. Relief poured from his heart like a tidal wave.

"Gods, you're alive. You're alive," he murmured, rocking the four-year-old back and forth.

The boy's face was covered in soot. The spy quickly checked him, but apart from a few minor scrapes, he was unharmed. His heart sank. He touched his son's damp hair and the wet blankets. Margaret had saved him, likely fighting off the raiders, and ensuring that he'd been in the safe room when the beam fell on her.

He should've been here. She shouldn't have had to fight them off, shouldn't have died.

"Is Mama okay?" the boy asked.

The spy's heart collapsed in on itself as grief ripped into his chest as surely as a raider's ax. The boy blinked, wiping the soot from his face. His lip shook.

He already knows.

The spy held him tighter and pressed a kiss to the boy's grimy forehead. "No, son, she's not. She loved you very much and gave her life to save you."

"She's... she's dead?" The boy's eyes watered, and his small shoulders shook.

"Let's go say goodbye."

He carried his wife into the garden. The boy pressed his face against his mother's chest and sobbed. The spy patted his son's back for a long time, but they couldn't stay here forever. Finally, he buried her deep in the garden. He placed a large rock upon her grave, a final goodbye to the woman he'd loved.

Grief and anger warred in his heart as his son laid flowers atop his mother's grave.

The godsdamned in-fighting and raids of this cursed continent. This never should've happened. The greedy kings and war tribes. Always fighting. Borders changed. People died. And it went round and round again. The cycle that never stopped. The spy gritted his teeth. He was done with it. They wouldn't stay in Demorra another day, and he refused to serve kings who didn't deserve it.

He'd heard stories from travelers about a land without fighting and greed. It was worth finding out whether the stories were true.

He touched his son's shoulder. "Let's salvage what we can of our things. We have a long journey ahead."

"Where are we going?"

"Avyllon."

His son tilted his head. "Why Avyllon?"

"I've heard stories about their Goddess. She sees all—past, present, and future. She loves her people and does not allow them to starve or fight."

"Will you spy for Avyllon?"

The spy's features hardened, and he gently squeezed his son's small hand. "I'd like nothing more than to see all of Demorra burn."

New Mission

Chapter One

Never step into a shadow atop dark, still water when the moon is gone, or you could lose your soul.

— *Warning given to shepherds, sentinels, and spies.*

1152 N.T.C. Fifty-five years later. The city of Rexila, the heart of the Demorran Empire, named for the Grand Imperial Emperor Jhames Edwyrd Alexandir Rexil, the Wolf, Moon-blessed, conqueror of seventeen kingdoms, and favorite son of the Lunar Goddess Niamh.

The nameless one learned his given name when he was eight years old. It was the first and last time he'd heard it. The best spies remained nameless, faceless, until death. His grandfather and father managed it in Avyllon's service—and he'd be godsdamned if he wouldn't live up to that.

Infiltrating somewhere as immense as the imperial palace in Rexila was simpler than one might imagine. It required knowing when to trick a person, or when a stroke of ink on a stolen paper would be stamped without a second look. Turning a seven into an eight on the number of guards stationed in the throne room was too easy. One of the workers in the bakery where he was assigned agreed to cover for him today because he'd claimed he needed to care for an ailing grandparent, which gave him his alibi.

The clay from Nucifera's lotus lake he'd used to reshape his features into something older than his twenty-odd years tickled his nose. *Gods of death*, he wanted to scratch it so badly he was about to lose his shadow-cursed mind, but he couldn't risk unsticking his false nose. He scanned the imperial throne room, wondering whether the other guards would notice. One guard shifted his weight from foot to foot, and the eyes of the others snapped to him.

They'd notice.

And now his ears itched under the clay. *Focus on* anything *else*. He ran through what he'd learned since arriving in Demorra in an attempt to distract himself from the itch that threatened to undo him. He'd written to Avyllon's High Seer a few times in the last two weeks since he'd stumbled into a warehouse incinerating corpses subjected to failed magical experiments. Aurienne had replied in coded messages that they were the Mooncursed of legend.

He'd snuck into the city's main library to see if there was any information on the Mooncursed. Only a few fairytales remained. Many books had been *removed*. From what he could piece together, the Mooncursed were reminiscent of werewolves, but unlike werewolves, they weren't bound to the changes of the moon. They remained frozen in the werewolf transformation, more wolf than human. Raving beasts who cared only for the hunt and the kill. He flexed his jaw. Those books were somewhere. Probably in this palace, locked away.

More information was needed to send back to the High Seer. A map. A letter. List of resources. Troop locations. He'd take anything. Glancing around, he studied the enormous columns carved into fire-breathing dragons and covered in crushed pearls that reflected the fading afternoon light. His eyes trailed to the ancient throne carved from black titan ore metal flecked with diamond and gold.

A bead of sweat slipped between the stitched seam of his long, black wig and down the back of his neck. The padding he wore to simulate the bulky muscles on his shoulders was hot, smelled mildly of button quail feathers, and was *itchy*. His feet sweated atop the wool-wrapped lifts in his shoes.

Shadows of Nyx'ela, why was it so hot in this room?

Rexila was traditionally cooler than Avyllon, and after spending months in tropical Arryn, he shouldn't be sweating like this. And winter was only about a month away. He glanced across the mosaic floors at another guard. Sweat pooled beneath the man's arms. It was strangely hot in this room, even for the other guards.

Why?

The throne room had been empty since his post began an hour ago. In fact, the only strange thing was that *nothing* had happened. The emperor hadn't appeared. If he wasn't here, where was he?

Unease pooled in the nameless one's stomach. Avyllon's summit was scheduled for today. He'd never learned whether Aurienne had convinced the allies to attend. Had the emperor learned of the summit?

Metallic growls reverberated through the hallway leading to the imperial administrative chambers. Scraping. Thumping. Heavy breathing. Something was approaching, and he meant some*thing*. He knew what they were before they even entered the room.

Mooncursed.

His face grew cold as the blood rushed to his frantically pumping heart. A man strode into the throne room, holding the end of a thick metal leash. Eryx, the emperor's advisor. The leash dragged on the floor, scraping and squealing against the brilliant tiles. Behind him, a deformed, wretched creature limped in. One leg was partially covered in fur, revealing forged metal inside. Rows of broken fangs jutted out from a gaping mouth. It wore a metal collar, and black blood seeped from the inward-facing spikes. The black metal was sparkled with gold and diamond fragments—the same as the throne.

The snarling beast unspooled terror inside him. Soldiers couldn't stand up against a beast like this. They'd be mowed down by the hundreds. Nothing could defeat this. It would end Avyllon and then the rest of the continent.

Eryx dragged five Mooncursed to the center of the room. Dozens more lurked behind him, with hulking wardens holding their leashes. The beasts snarled at the quivering guards. One lunged at him and snapped its teeth. An acrid smell wafted from the creature's mouth.

"Get over here," Eryx grated, yanking on the chain.

Tensing every muscle in his body to keep from reacting, the nameless one checked his periphery to ascertain what the other guards were doing. They didn't abandon their posts but did glance around with wide eyes. It meant they'd never seen the creatures either but were too afraid to react. He furrowed his brow in the same unspoken questions as the others to not stand out.

Snarls filled the air with a dull roar. So many monsters. The spy found it hard to breathe.

The emperor entered the room in purple and gold robes and a dark expression. He lifted his hands and purple light glowed in his palms.

"Let's see how their resistance fares when faced with the might of the empire," the emperor said.

Boom.

A fissure of light ripped through the air. Several guards lifted their arms and shielded their eyes from the blinding light. The nameless one didn't move. A combination of training and shock froze him into place.

The emperor stepped through the Way followed by guards and priestess of Niamh—marked as such by the glowing metal ring burned into their foreheads behind their veils. The Way closed behind them.

Minutes passed, and the spy's collar grew drenched in sweat as he hardly dared to breathe. Mooncursed snarled, waiting, pacing. The nameless one tried to think. Ways were only used by powerful sorcerers and only at the Way gates to connect to other Ways.

Holy eyes of Nyx'ela, the emperor opened a Way in the middle of the room. He... could open them on command.

The Way opened again.

The wardens released the Mooncursed, and they poured through the Way. Wardens followed, and screams and clanging steel echoed from the other side.

Dozens of beasts charged through the Way, followed by their handlers. The spy glanced at the other guards and at the Way. Even if he were to do something, what could he do against these beasts? Shouting and chaos spilled over.

The spy fingered his ornamental weapons. The fighting continued for long minutes as shouting, screaming, and snarling echoed through the Way. Demorran soldiers poured through. Battle raged on the other side, but the spy didn't know enough to do anything and was vastly outnumbered.

Emperor Rexil retreated back through, robes whipping in wind from the powerful magic. His emissary and a dozen injured wardens and a handful of priestesses followed. Several Mooncursed followed, bleeding and howling.

The spy stared ahead, forcing himself to rely on his training.

"That godsdamned seer!" the emperor shouted.

The nameless one tracked the emperor's angry tirade toward the large carved map of the Demorran empire. He carefully catalogued the new information. The Way. Mooncursed beasts. The emperor. Niamh's priestesses.

Aurienne had informed him that the Demorran emissary wasn't aware that the monument-based magical portals sorcerers opened, called Ways, could be used for travel. Yet, the emperor opened and closed this one at will. Did he even realize what magic he wielded? Ancient, forgotten magic—and if the tomes were to be believed—there was always a deep cost for such magic.

"What happened?" Eryx and Emissary Seiko shadowed the emperor toward the throne.

The emperor gripped the hand rests of the throne, before turning to take his seat. "The High Seer knew about Niamh."

The nameless one tried his best to gauge the reactions of the advisors. They froze and might have paled. It was hard to tell with his eyes trained forward.

"What did they know?"

"Enough for me to know there's a spy in Demorra," the emperor snarled.

Oh, god of hells.

His skin prickled. More sweat trickled down his wig seam, and his muscles screamed from the uncomfortable disguise, but he refused to move, refused to breathe. His feet were already bruised, his legs hurt, and his nose still *itched*. But he couldn't afford to draw any attention.

"She couldn't possibly know—" Emissary Seiko was cut off.

"She knows more than she should," Emperor Rexil interrupted. "Her sight should have been limited. Our plans should have been veiled. We ensured it. Somehow, she's managed to break through the spells."

His mind grasped at threads of information that flew into the darkness.

"Damn her to the darkest hells. May all the gods of Nyx'ela consume her wretched soul," the emperor snarled.

The nameless one watched closely. Sweat stained the robes under the emperor's arms and along his chest. His face was pale, and bags were already darkening his eyes. He didn't look this ragged minutes ago.

Opening the Ways must weaken him.

The emperor sagged against the winged throne. "I used a considerable amount of stored energy to open that Way against Niamh's instruction. I won't be able to open another one for some time."

Eryx gripped the Mooncursed's leash. "Is it because of the—"

The emperor hurled a chalice against the columns and wine splashed against tapestries.

"Yes," the emperor hissed. "And if someone doesn't find me that map *now*, I am going to start sending people to meet the gods of death by the dozen. I need that map to find what prevents me from using Niamh's magic there. I must destroy it."

That caught the spy's attention. Whatever the emperor searched for was the sole thing preventing him from invading, keeping his magic at bay. If the emperor found the map showing where it was and his magic was no longer limited, he'd be unstoppable. The nameless one couldn't let the emperor get his hands on it.

The nameless one's hand twitched for his concealed dagger. The emperor was so close. One well-placed throw and the threat would vanish. He glanced at the Mooncursed, the soldiers, the guards, and the priestesses. He'd be dead before the knife left his hand, and if the emperor could open a Way, then he might have magics he wasn't aware of. The nameless one needed to bide his time and gather more information.

One of the priestesses was shaking her head and rubbing her eyes. She blinked hard and touched the glowing white ring in her forehead. *That's odd.* The priestesses never seemed aware of their surroundings. They were usually caught in a fog or dream. She squeezed her hand and winced.

Eryx toyed with the metal leash as if a five-hundred-pound beast wasn't at the other end. "We have leads on several ancient maps we think might note the location you requested. We're tracking them down now."

Not if I find it first.

Inside, the nameless one smiled. He'd learned more than he ever dreamed. As long as he survived the exit, he had everything he needed. He'd find that map and figure out what it had to do with Niamh and the emperor's magic.

"Prepare all our armies. Once we have that map, we'll invade," the emperor snapped.

Two decades of training couldn't keep the spy's eyes from widening. The satisfaction was ripped away as his heart twisted into an ugly knot. His hands shook at his sides, and he couldn't trust himself to breathe without gasping. Invade. The might of all the nations of Demorra were preparing to invade. And with the Mooncursed... How could Teridar stand against them?

Eryx bowed. "The armies await your command. They could be across the isthmus and into Avyllon in a fortnight."

The spy fought the urge to swallow. The armies were mobilized. He had to get word to Aurienne, to warn her. Alone. The nameless one had his new mission—delay the invasion by whatever means necessary, which meant learning more about the Mooncursed. And first, to do so, he needed to find that map and steal it, so the emperor couldn't find whatever kept him weak.

The emperor slammed his fist against the metal throne. "And someone hunt down that godsdamned spy and bring me his head."

TAPESTRIES
CHAPTER TWO

Eight hours later, the nameless one strode away from the palace toward the local tavern. Several imperial guards tucked their hats under their arms, others shook out the tension from their long shift.

"Night shift is the worst. I'm left drinking with you lot because all the women have gone home." A guard nudged another playfully.

"Not that it'd make a difference, you're going home alone either way," the nameless one taunted.

That brought laughs from a dozen others.

The nameless one slung his arm around the man's shoulders, thanking his shoe lifts for the ability to do so. "There's not enough rice wine in the empire to tempt 'em."

The man laughed and shoved him off. "We'll see who's going home alone tonight! Who wants to put a bet on it?"

Several guards jostled forward with coins in hand, and the nameless one allowed himself to fall into the pack. He'd spent the last two weeks loitering in the taverns the guards frequented to become a familiar face. The uniform was easy enough to obtain from a laundress, and then it was about making just enough of an impression to be remembered—but never missed.

"Was anyone in the throne room when the emperor returned?" a slender, female guard called out. "Now that was some godscursed magic, if I've ever seen it."

The statement stalled the spy's departure.

"Then you've not had to guard the shrine," a man at the back snorted. "The screams echo through those stone walls loud enough you're deaf for days."

The spy drifted toward the man. Gods—he wanted to ask questions, but people remembered questions. Better to wait and listen.

A tall woman—a Khesrossi, from the long brown hair—said, "I heard Huan vomited all over the floors, and Eryx removed him from the detail immediately. You've got to have a strong stomach for that place."

"I'd rather do that than work the incinerator with those mountains of corpses," a man said.

Another man nudged the other, hard. "Shut it, that's confidential."

The incinerator must be the place I stumbled upon two weeks ago with all the Mooncursed corpses. And the shrine... must be where they create them. Where Eryx helps to create them. Where could that be?

Once the nameless one found the map to keep the emperor's magic weak, he had to stop the creation of the Mooncursed beasts. He added it to his growing list of tasks.

"Why were there eight of us in the throne room today? There are only seven exits," someone called.

That was fast. He hoped they'd find the clerical error and believe it to be the slip of a pen, nothing more. They still might, but it was time to go before anyone asked any pressing questions. Besides—he had a map to find.

The first of the guards reached the tavern. The nameless one watched for an opening. Waiting for the moment when all the eyes were elsewhere, he stepped into a shadow. He flipped his coat around and tugged open the hood. Discarding the quail feathers simulating the bulk of muscles into a garbage bin, he slipped the lifts from his dress shoes and took a very different shape. With a single motion, he wiped all the disguise clay from his face—and finally was able to scratch his nose.

Shadows and shades, that was amazing.

He audibly groaned as he tore the wig from his head and stuffed everything into a raggedy bag. He slipped the beggar's bowl from his hat and dumped the coins within. The entire process took just a few moments.

Then, he limped down the road. He paused to watch the guards fill the bar with roaring laughs and splashing wine. He'd joined and left groups just like this one a hundred, a thousand, times before, disappearing without a trace. Tonight, a pang crossed his chest. Frozen in place, he listened to the loud stories, wishing for once he could stay.

He shouldered the ragged cloak and tore his gaze away. After this mission, he needed a long break and a visit with his mother. The loneliness of the job was getting to him, and that was dangerous.

His rented apartment was across the city, but it gave him precious time to think. The army could be in Avyllon in a fortnight. Something was keeping the emperor's magic weak, some ancient location marked on old maps. And there was still the issue of the mobilized army *and* the Mooncursed beasts.

A baker walked across his path—Jun. His fellow baker who'd covered for him today at work. He stepped into a shadow and swept the beggar's clothes from his back. He tucked them into a grocery bag he removed from the sole of his shoe. Now wearing the normal, albeit sweaty, clothes he'd worn under his imperial uniform all day.

"Jun!" he called, waving.

Jun turned, wiping his hands on his flour-caked apron. "Feng, how are your grandparents?"

Feng—one of the hundreds of aliases he'd created as a child. He slipped into them like his disguises and shed them as easily.

He lifted the grocery bag. "Much better. I'll make up the loaves tomorrow for quota."

"No, no," Jun said. "Don't you even think on it. We handled it."

"I will make them up tomorrow. I promise. Even if just for someone else," the spy pressed.

The Feng persona wouldn't allow a debt to go unpaid, and it didn't sit well with *him* either.

"If you want." Jun held out an herbed loaf. "Here, take this. We were given a few loaves to take home. Give it to your grandparents."

A rumble in his stomach silenced the refusal on his lips. He had nothing for supper, and it'd been a long night.

He accepted it and forced a smile. "Thanks. See you tomorrow."

Waving, the spy strode underneath the bright firefly lanterns lighting his way home. Dawn brightened the imperial city where its inhabitants were just beginning to wake. Thank the gods of Nyx'ela that today was his one day off, else he'd already have to be at the bakery.

The nameless one climbed three flights of stairs then pushed open the creaky wooden door to his small apartment. His drooping eyelids demanded sleep. Just a few hours and then he'd begin fresh.

A letter with the High Seer's small moon sigil traced in the corner was wedged under his door. He snatched it up and broke the seal. Skimming the coded letter, he pieced together the message. The emperor was preparing to invade Avyllon. Well, he'd gleaned as much from the emperor's reaction earlier, and new information likely wouldn't be coming for a week.

He rubbed his neck and held the letter over the flame but stopped. Faint letters pressed into the paper caught his attention.

A second message?

He threw open a drawer and several buttons and a ball of yarn rolled inside. Hastily, he dug through the odds and ends until he found a charcoal stick. Returning to the candle, he carefully rubbed the charcoal against the paper until the letters appeared.

This world makes monsters of us all.

He sat heavily on a hard wooden chair. That wasn't any code they'd agreed on. A mistake? The High Seer wasn't one to make mistakes. Everything she did was intentional. Planned. Meticulous. She'd never send a false message without meaning to. What could it mean?

He checked the paper for any other messages, but that was all it said. Clicking his teeth, he held the paper over the fire.

Staring out the grimy window, he bit into the soft flesh of the loaf.

Perfectly baked and still warm. The herbs exploded in his mouth, and there was a hint of chicken broth—tricking his stomach into believing he was eating meat.

Just a few hours of sleep, and he'd start hunting for the map. He scrubbed the clay and other paint from his body and carefully washed the disguises. Setting them out to dry, he finally succumbed to his drooping eyelids. His head settled onto the lumpy pillow as he pulled the threadbare blankets up to his chin. Sleep came quickly in his too-silent room.

One hundred and seventy-three mapmakers resided in the imperial city of Rexila. The spy knew because he'd been to every godsdamned one of them over the past few days. Of those, only thirty-one had maps of Avyllon, and they were all current. None showed magic or gods or history of any sort eluding to any unknown, ancient monuments or artifacts. He approached his twelfth antiques dealer of the day, wearing his twenty-second disguise. His stomach rumbled, he was dusty, and his left heel was bruised. He'd been trailing a few of the emperor's soldiers searching for the map, staying ahead of as many as he could. So far, they hadn't found it either.

The foretelling Rite showed Aurienne he would destroy their continent—but why? What would he gain? It made no sense.

Bam. Bam. Bam. An imperial guard pounded his fist on a nearby door. "Open up."

A slight man opened the door and was ripped into the street. He bounced off his knees on the knobby cobblestones. Guards pushed inside the house.

"Your offering bowl has gone empty for a week. You know the emperor's law," the imperial guard on the street said.

The spy kept his head down, listening carefully. He glanced at the purple stone bowl that sat beside every house in the city. How did the guards know? He doubted anyone from the neighborhood would have snitched.

"I swear I've been leaving offerings," the man said.

"There's an altar to Dhagaos in here," a guard said as he returned to the street. "It was covered in candles."

The guards turned their stony gazes upon the man. "I leave them for both!"

"A night in the dungeons will remind you of your duty to Niamh," a guard said.

"My wife has passed away, and I have two children," the man exclaimed.

The guard's face softened for half a second. "I'll give you a few moments to find someone they can stay with tonight."

Gritting his teeth, the spy forced himself to keep walking. Anger coursed through him, but there was nothing he could do. Niamh wasn't a goddess he'd heard of before the last few weeks. The emperor had mentioned her, and he'd overheard people talking, but she was not part of the pantheon his father had taught him before he and Grandfather left Demorra for Avyllon. There was something strange going on with this new goddess.

The nameless one was near the antiquity vendor when another disturbance stopped him.

"It's priceless! You can't have it," the vendor was shouting. "That's a five-hundred-year-old map of Teridar."

Several imperial guards struggled to roll up a large tapestry and wrap it in a thick wool covering.

Hells.

The spy slowly backed out and turned toward an adjacent booth and pretended to inspect specialty crane quills and lotus flower inks. While nodding politely at the booth owner, he was listening keenly.

Thud.

"Here's payment for the tapestry." The guard slammed a bag of gold at the map owner's feet. "More than double what it's worth. The emperor is fair and just."

"That's an heirloom. It can't be replicated," the owner wailed.

"Stand aside, sir, or we'll move you," a guard snapped.

Four guards strained under the weight of the wall-sized tapestry as they filed out of the shop.

"Move! By order of the emperor," they shouted. "Out of the way."

The spy trailed them, keeping to the shadows and side roads. Watching. A dozen guards escorted the tapestry—the map.

He wracked his brain. *Think, think, what can I do to take it?* But it was so heavy, he'd never be able to carry it on his own even if he got it away from them. He had nothing to switch it out with without more planning, and there was no time. If the emperor even saw the location of what he sought, he wouldn't need the map anymore.

The only option was to watch where they took it and to try to get it from there. At a safe distance a street over, he followed.

They walked it up to the entrance of the palace. The gates shut behind them, as the spy lingered in the shadows. He'd studied the layout of the palace for weeks and knew there were only three places they'd take it. The throne room, the vault, or one of the libraries.

He had to get to that map before the emperor, so the monuments remained lost. If the emperor found what he sought, he'd be unstoppable.

Infiltration
Chapter Three

Muttering curses, the spy crept through the seventh library in the palace. He'd snuck in minutes after the guards brought the map in. Usually preferring weeks of planning, he'd had no time. This mission, he'd have to improvise. He couldn't allow the emperor to find the location of what he sought, so he'd used pieces of other planned missions to sneak in and luck had been on his side. The nameless one still didn't have a strategy for how to get the tapestry out. He continued the search.

The throne room was easy to check, and he'd discovered that the vault hadn't been opened in days. That left the unending libraries tucked away in every corridor. It made no sense. He'd been studying the emperor's movements and personality for weeks. He'd read everything he could, asked about him, listened. He'd mapped out the entire palace to infiltrate it. There was nowhere else...

What in all the hells? Where could it be?

Think. The emperor demanded the map. It was important to him. It stood between him invading Teridar, and he sounded desperate to destroy it. Something marked on the map was protecting Teridar, and it had power over him. Where else would he have put it?

Unless... No. He wouldn't. Would he?

It was in the emperor's chambers. It had to be. Where else would he keep something so precious? He'd want it nearby so he could study it at all hours.

The nameless one froze. Breaking into the emperor's private chambers would be no easy feat, even with all the planning to infiltrate the palace. He slipped out of the library and down the halls. Night had descended upon the city as he darted from shadow to shadow. An open window on the floor below the emperor's bedroom was the only way up.

Flexing his fingers, he started to climb. The cracks in the mortar were hardly wide enough for a fingertip, but he'd been climbing sheer cliffs since he was a child. Very few people could make the climb, and none would dare this high above the ground. The lower levels offered better handholds, but this high up, the walls were polished smooth.

He'd scoped out this path for a possible assassination attempt if the High Seer ordered one, but the emperor was always surrounded by guards, advisors, sometimes Mooncursed, sorcerers, and poison tasters. He'd abandoned the idea as nearly impossible, but the path into the room worked well if it was empty.

Pressing his body to the wall, he pulled himself up onto the balcony quietly. This one balcony was four times larger than the spy's apartment, and the emperor's chambers had *three* balconies this size. The room was dark, save for the blazing fireplace and a few dim firefly lanterns. It looked empty. Twenty minutes later, he finally picked all the locks and slipped in through a window. Thank X'era, the guards were posted outside the room.

The tapestry hung from the ceiling on a wall in front of the four-poster bed. He paused, relief flooding through him at finally finding it. Now... what to do with it. The thing was absolutely massive. If it fell from the metal hanging clips, it could crush him.

It was beautiful though.

The nameless one stood before the wall-height tapestry depicting the continent of Teridar. Gilded, tightly woven, and stained with deep, rich colors, it was *old*. The purple mountains and rosy lakes remained, but all the cities and borders had shifted. And there were large blue monuments marked all over. Monuments he'd never seen before. He tried to memorize every landmark, but it was so detailed and different.

Worse—he had no idea what specifically the emperor was looking for.

It could be anything.

Voices approached from the hall. The clicking of the guards' boots told him they snapped to attention. His heart raced as his adrenaline spiked. He needed to hide *now*.

He glanced under the bed, but immediately discarded the idea. It was the first place a person looked when searching a room. He'd only use it in a last resort. He slipped into a cabinet, glancing through the slats as he waited for the voices to quiet. The door opened and the slippered shuffling of several scholarly types filed in.

"They are here! The map has them all. We'll make a note of locations and send scouts at once," one scholar said.

The spy strained to listen from behind the clothes inside the cabinet.

"We'll wait for the emperor's orders. He should be returning from the shrine soon. He was pleased that the map had been found," another said.

Time was running out.

The scholars filed out of the emperor's chambers. Minutes passed and no one else entered the room. The guards talked in low voices in the hall, and the emperor could be returning any minute. The nameless one didn't like to work when he could be overheard, but he was running out of time. He'd have to risk it.

Now or never.

Peering out of the cabinet, he locked eyes with a woman looking out from under the bed.

Nearly falling backward into the cabinet, he bit down on a gasp, eyes widening at the intruder. The *other* intruder. She stared, her own eyes widening, and her mouth falling open.

Gods of Nyx'ela.

What was she doing here? How had she gotten in? How long had she been here? Her expression narrowed into a glare—as if he was somehow inconveniencing her.

"What are you doing here?" she mouthed, her lips snapping through the words like a whip cracking bottles.

He pointed to his chest, brows raised, before pointing back at her. "What are *you* doing here?"

She was going to get them both caught, and if the guards found them in here, there would be no trial. They'd be executed before the sun went down. He swallowed. And then no one would save Avyllon from these beasts.

She waved her arm in the sweeping, wild motions one might use to fend off a Meili'de grizzly.

"You leave," he mouthed in return, waving his arm at her from inside the narrow cupboard.

She raised a single finger at him and wagged it, mouthing more words he couldn't understand.

He caught, "I was here first," and then it devolved into a string of curses.

How dare she?

He pressed his finger to his lips. For the love of all the gods, he wished she'd stay quiet.

He pointed at her angrily. "Get out."

She waved again, snarling. "You."

This was juvenile. It was incredibly unprofessional. His father would be ashamed, and his grandfather would be rolling in his grave. But she was going to ruin everything.

And then she closed her hand into a fist, twisted the fingers of her other hand, and made one of the crudest gestures he'd ever seen.

His mouth dropped open. Despite their dire circumstances, he was shocked.

How... rude.

She grinned, crossing her arms and placing her chin on her hands underneath the bed like a cat sunning itself on a windowsill.

Except, he'd been drinking with Aurienne once or twice between missions, and he'd learned the gesture to end all gestures. It was more of a story, with a plot, character arc, and theme. Six hand positions later, he'd wiped the smug smile off her face. Her mouth hung open—probably not wise what with the rodents he'd seen in some of the adjoining rooms—and she pressed up on her elbows, a mix of confusion, offense, and shock flashing on her face. She blinked hard, glanced at him, and then blinked again, as if trying to process what she'd seen.

You'll be figuring out the mechanics of that one for days to come.

The spy ignored her and listened for any sounds in the hall. Nothing. The guards were gone. He stepped out of the cupboard and crossed his arms. She froze—as if suddenly remembering why she was here. And he'd love to know why that was. She slithered out from under the bed.

She wore a maid's uniform—gray apron atop a simple gray dress. Her hair was pulled back into a braid. *First mistake.* The maids kept their hair cropped short to keep from getting caught in the furnace or laundry soaps. Her boots were wrong—the maids wore soft-soled slippers. *Second mistake.* She was beautiful, too beautiful to avoid notice. Perfect, porcelain skin. Shiny black hair. Delicately slender as a pole—perfect for espionage. She should have given herself a false nose or wart or anything to obscure her beauty. *Third mistake.*

"What are you doing here?" she hissed.

He held up a hand. "Shush."

"Don't shush me," she snapped.

"If you had any idea what you were doing, I wouldn't have to."

She opened her mouth and then closed it. She glanced toward the tapestry. "I'm here for that."

It was no use lying. He'd been caught—but at least he was wearing a decent disguise. He would just shift aliases and use another backstory she'd believe. He could turn this around. And to start, he'd give her a sliver of truth.

"Me too."

Side by side, they studied the tapestry.

"What... what do you want it for?" She stuffed her hands into her apron and glanced his way.

He wasn't about to tell her anything remotely true.

"To sell it."

Her brows pulled together. "You did all this just to sell it?"

The real question was why did she want it? That's what he had to figure out before answering. If she was willing to sneak in here, she wasn't loyal to the emperor. A rebel maybe? Or a thief. A rebel wouldn't want the emperor to have it either. A thief would want to take it for herself. If he played this right, he could get her to help him steal it and then conveniently make it disappear.

Voices echoed in the hall. "Fine! You can sell it," she whispered. "After we copy it."

"Fine."

She took a deep breath. "How are we going to get it out?"

That was the question he'd been wrestling with ever since he'd followed those guards from the antiquities dealer's shop.

"It took four of them to carry," he mused. "I don't know how we're going to get it out of here, especially not unseen. Even if the two of us managed to carry it..."

The emperor's voice sounded in the hall. "Show me."

Godsdamn it.

His adrenaline spiked again as his skin prickled with warning. He glanced around the room. He could hide the map under the bed, but it would likely be found on the next clean. They could toss it out the window, but the guards below would just snatch it. There was no way to get it out. His eyes fell upon the lit fireplace.

There was only one option.

Better for no one to have those locations than for the emperor to have them. If the emperor found what he sought, they'd be doomed. The spy had to destroy the map.

Her eyes followed his to the fire. Their gazes met again. The room burst into motion all at once.

"No," she cried.

He darted for a burning log and pulled it free. She darted in front of him, but he reached around her and touched the log to the tapestry.

It caught flame.

"He can't have this," the nameless one said.

He dragged the burning log down the tapestry, scorching all the major landmarks.

The door burst open for the emperor and guards to see a maid protecting the tapestry from a would-be thief or assassin. It couldn't have been better timing if he'd planned it. She'd be fine, and he'd be gone. He darted toward the window.

"Catch him!" The emperor's face bulged with furious, purple veins.

The spy slipped out the window, dropped down onto the next balcony, and scrambled across the decorative stonework. He paused only to flip his cloak so the side matching the stonework faced out. The emperor leaned out the window—but the spy was already gone.

The witching hour fell upon the city, when the night grew too quiet, and reality warped. Shadows stretched long in the blinking firefly lantern light. Puddles were inky and dark, and far too inhabited. The wind blew a little too softly. The waning moon hung over the city, closer than usual and nearly full. It took up the entire sky.

He'd been leaning against the wall for about an hour. Guilt had kept him haunting the palace, waiting for the woman to leave. He'd circled the exits several times, sure he hadn't missed her yet. If they released her, it would be out this one. They must still be questioning her, or they made her return to her shift. If she didn't come out by morning, he'd have to figure out a way to free her from the dungeons. For reasons he didn't want to explore, he couldn't leave her in his mess even if he knew he should.

His heart rate slowed to near that of slumber as he steadied his breathing. His eyes were half-lidded, willing himself to blend into his surroundings. He detached from his body as his limbs fell away. One with the shadows. In moments like these, he felt like he could truly disappear. One man walked right past him and never once looked in his direction. Maybe he was invisible.

Drip.

Drip.

Drip.

Water from one of the city's many collection vessels dripped into a puddle beside him. Somewhere a baby was cooing softly. A dog barked.

Drip.

Drip.

Drip.

The door opened and the woman walked out. Tension unspooled from his chest.

Thank the gods.

She looked around cautiously. Looking for him? He owed her an explanation. Maybe? No. He should just leave it alone. She was safe, and he had work to do. She paused, scanning the night. Could she sense him? He hesitated. If today was any indication, he couldn't stop the emperor alone. Maybe she could help? If she wanted to thwart the emperor... he could use allies. Maybe she knew about the shrine, incinerator, or Mooncursed. He didn't have the map, and he needed information desperately.

Blanketed in darkness, he weighed the options. His tasks were too great to accomplish alone, and as much as he hated to admit it, he could use some help. Or was that just the loneliness talking? Although, if she'd made it all the way into the emperor's chambers, she must have some useful connections, even if her disguises could use work. She might not be a born spy, but right now, she was his best option. He pushed off the wall into the light. She glanced his way, locking eyes with him.

That was when the night changed.

Silence fell.

The collection vessel ceased dripping into the wide puddle, and the gloomy water grew still as glass. The wind died. A black cloud passed in front of the looming moon, shrouding the city.

The spy shuddered, feeling icy needles dance down his spine. A warning that he'd learned not to ignore. He needed to get to the woman and get them both somewhere safe, now. Danger lurked on these streets. Magic.

The nameless one took a step toward her, right into the inky, swirling shadows of the puddle—and fell.

BETWEEN WORLDS
CHAPTER FOUR

The nameless one fell through inky water. Down and down, he was dragged into the depths, and just as he could hold his breath no longer, he fell out the bottom of an ocean and into golden-lined clouds. Lungs burning, he gasped for air.

Dozens of dusky red and orange moons orbited the starless skies in the floating ocean. The deafening, crashing waves surrounded him. Rainbow fish with mirrored scales and delicate fins flipped through the spiraling waves high above. Mauve lotus flowers twisted in the air beside floating strands of pearls.

He bounced off a pastel pink cloud into another and bounced again. There was no up or down, and yet he was falling through the shadows of endless worlds. Gilded mirrors suspended in the clouds opened doorways into the worlds beyond the veil—the worlds the seers always spoke of. He'd somehow fallen through one.

Am I dead?

Ribbons taller than trees stretched for leagues into the sky—purples and blues. He reached for one, feeling the silky fabric brush against his fingers. It exploded into a thousand jeweled butterflies. The butterflies swarmed him, biting and scratching, drawing blood. He shouted, but the endless worlds consumed the noise. Grasping one of the butterflies, he crunched down on it with his teeth. Hissing, they flew away through one of the mirrors, causing the surface to ripple like water.

He dropped through the pastel clouds and fell between the floating islands. Waterfalls poured water from mountain lakes, which splashed into islands below—like the endless fountains in Avyllon. One island crashed into another, raining down debris. He shielded his face, and pebbles peppered his skin, leaving bruises and welts. This place was dangerous as it was beautiful.

As he fell through another layer of clouds, the ground appeared beneath him, coming up fast. He braced for the certain death that would accompany meeting the ground after so long. Squeezing his eyes shut, he prayed to the gods of Nyx'ela. The air rushed in his ears, and he knew the end would come soon.

His feet lightly touched down, and he cracked open an eye. A world-sized storm cloud crackled with lightning and thunder in the distance. Moons and planets danced above his head.

Where am I?

White mist swirled on the glimmering stones beneath his feet. The stones were pearly, and more precisely carved than even Demorra's ancient golden road—and it stretched on forever in every direction. Portals made for god-sized beings shimmered, set equidistant from one another. The towering portal doorframes were wrapped in vines or flowers, gargoyles or statues. Others had runes or ancient letters.

They were every color—but all the same general shape and size.

Ways? Could they be Ways? But this... this would let people travel between worlds.

"Hello?"

His voice echoed off the towering doorways. He'd been too surprised and shocked to feel much fear whilst falling, but now... Fear gripped his spine with icy fingers and his heart hammered loudly. He was all alone. Running to one of the doorways, he pressed his hand against the swirling lights.

Locked.

He ran to another door and another. All locked. They would not let him pass. He was well and truly trapped.

No. This can't be.

"Hello!"

Terror set in, and he hammered his fist against the translucent center of the doorways—seeing the strange creatures and landscapes on the other side that were sealed from him.

He was going to die here, alone, in this strange place. If he wasn't dead already.

"Is anyone there?" he called.

Only the rumbling storms replied. He sank to his knees, the hard, smooth stone biting into his kneecaps. Would he spend the rest of his days searching for a single open doorway? He looked up. Would he wait for his body to die so that he could float upwards through the world he'd fallen through?

Bowing his head, he tried to think. He'd never spent much time praying. His father and grandfather had always urged him to pray to all the gods residing in the mountains of Nyx'ela—especially death and shadows. He'd left offerings. He'd said a short prayer before every mission—but in this moment, he was ready to believe in true miracles. If only they could save him.

He pressed his palms together to pray. "Gods and goddesses of Nyx'ela, home of the gods. God of death and goddess of shadows. Please hear me. I need your aid. I am lost."

Tears dripped down his face as he fought to accept his fate. It couldn't end like this. Studying his hand, he realized that it was beginning to fade. It flickered in and out of existence.

No.

"Is anyone out there?" he whispered.

He pressed his forehead to the stone, praying for any miracle.

A voice replied, everywhere all at once. "I am here."

Relief flooded him, along with a mix of apprehension and dread. He stood, eyes searching for the source of the voice.

"Can you help me?"

A woman materialized from nothing. She was twice as tall as him, with slitted pupils in her purple eyes and starlight white hair that brushed the ground. She wore a gown of living shadows, and her lithe limbs were too long for her body.

"Yes." Her voice hurt his mortal ears. "I came because you called. You prayed to the god of death, the goddess of shadows—and so I came."

The goddess of shadows? That means... X'era. His blood froze as he realized he was in the presence of the divine.

"I am."

She read my mind?

"Yes."

Tears welled in his eyes.

You came for me.

She inclined her head to see him, so far below her. "I would not refuse the devout, you who have worshiped the shadows and anonymity your entire life. You who pray with your acts even more than your words. My beloved son." She whispered his true name.

Gratitude flooded through him. He didn't deserve the attention of a goddess. He didn't deserve her time, and yet, she came for him. He'd spend the rest of his life trying to be worthy of it.

"Do you know where I am? Or why I am here?"

"I do. You spent too long living in shadows, too long pretending to be no one, that when a gap between the worlds opened you became shadows." She twisted her wrist and shadows from her gown danced around it.

"Became shadows? I don't understand."

"The old magic of your world has woken," she said. "The magic from when worlds were formed, and life first stirred. It wakes to protect itself, and it is impressionable. It changes to mirror you."

He gazed blankly upon the being. His brain fought to understand the knowledge from her lips, but he found himself utterly mortal.

X'era licked the points of her teeth. "The mortals who planted trees can magic them now. Those who mined the mountains became stone. Those who honored nature became witches while those who venerated knowledge became sorcerers. Those who sought the future became seers, like their Triple Goddess."

His brows rose at the mention of other gods. "You know her?"

"The goddess of the seers. Yes. She is strong but young. Only a single millennium. I've had affairs lasting that long, one with a delightful star. No, not the one you're used to, a devouring red giant that was ripped to pieces when his sun died. Glorious." X'era blinked, her dreamy gaze re-focusing. "I know all the gods of all the worlds."

And yet she was here with him.

He glanced around. "Am I dead?"

She cocked her head. "Mmmm, depends on what you mean by dead. If you mean that your soul has passed from your world through the veil into the worlds of souls, then yes. If you mean your corporeal form has expired and ceases to hold your soul? Then no. You brought your body with you, for as long as it lasts."

For as long as it lasts.

His eyes widened. "My body is dying?"

"Your vessel is not meant for the world of shadows and dreams. It is not meant for the world beyond the veils. If you do not return soon, your body shall cease to exist."

"Can you show me the way home?"

"It is why I came. Walk with me, little shade."

She took long, slow steps, pausing between each step for him to catch up. He looked up at her face, committing every detail to memory. Her skin was coated with purple shadows, and her gown glistened with twinkling lights. They walked for many hours. The way she kept glancing at him told him she had much easier methods of traveling and was walking so slowly for his sake.

"Your world is in danger," she said.

"From the emperor?" he asked.

"The one he serves. I know of Niamh, the one Demorra now worships." She snarled and the sky cracked. "She is no true god. She is a false goddess who will tear this world to pieces. You must stop her."

He touched his heart. "I will do all I can. I swear it."

"Good. Here is your door." She gestured to the door before them.

Orderly stacked stones were carved with wolves and dragons. It was inset with pearls and black diamonds and covered in runes. Lotus flowers bloomed on gilded vines. The seven phases of the moon crested the door's arch. It felt familiar at once, though he could have searched for lifetimes and never found it on his own.

"Thank you," he said.

"Take this ring."

She handed him a black metal ring flecked with gold and diamonds. Titan ore—he realized—swirled with some other unknown metal. The rune for her name, one he'd seen in the temples, was engraved into the top along with runes he didn't recognize. He took it carefully. Her fingers brushed against his, frigid as icicles. His body flared to life at her divine touch. Hands shaking, he slipped the ring onto his index finger.

She smiled with feline teeth. "It will keep you tethered to your world, and your world's shadow world. The magic of shadowstepping is yours. Shadows will serve as doorways in your world alone. You may step through them without fear of falling between worlds again so long as you wear my ring."

"Thank you. I will serve you every day of my life, I swear it."

X'era's voice was the last thing he heard before he stepped through the door. "Beware, little shade. If you stray too long in the shadows, your body will turn to smoke, and your soul will be all that remains."

Alter Egos

Chapter Six

Clad in a faded grayish apron tied over simple linen clothes, the spy jogged after his muttering coworker.

"Jun. Jun, wait," the spy called.

Jun whirled on him. "What." His flat tone was startling on his usually cheery demeanor.

"I'm sorry I was gone. Something unexpected came up and…"

"What came up?" Jun crossed his thick arms.

"I was… busy." He'd had all night to come up with a better excuse why Feng, his alter ego, would have missed work without telling anyone. Yet, guilt twisted his tongue.

"And you couldn't even let us know?" Jun snapped. "We had seven other people to cover for. And they let us know. They had reasons. Searching for missing family members. Rebuilding an exterior wall that had been destroyed in the night. Repairing their neighborhood well. And you were *busy*. That first day we missed quota."

The spy cringed. Missing quota was serious. People were imprisoned and terminated for much less. He'd only been in Demorra a few weeks, and even he knew that.

Jun exhaled. "We had to stay three hours late, and they still docked my pay. I didn't get to see my kids for two days, Feng."

The excuses died on the spy's lips. "It won't happen again. I swear it. I was—"

"Busy. Next time you want to get so drunk you disappear, do it on your day off."

They stepped inside the enormous factory with high ceilings and windows spanning the top of the walls. A woman passed the spy with a large, thick basket full of bread—casting a shadow over his feet. The shadow turned black and inky.

"Oh godsdamn it."

The nameless one's feet slipped through the shadow and tossed him out a shadow on the bakery's ceiling. He dropped nearly his entire height and landed in a pile on the floor behind Jun.

Jun turned to catch the spy scrambling to his feet. "What is wrong with you? Are you still... Never mind. From now on you're on your own. If you miss work no one will lie for you." He stormed away, shaking his head.

"Jun." He groaned.

He filed past the daily assignment board near the entrance and followed the others toward the kneading room. The room was lined with long, stone-topped tables with scales between every few people. His first loaf was set before him, and he began kneading. Narrowed gazes of other workers lingered on him.

This was bad. He couldn't afford this much attention right now. He'd have to find a way to fix this and avoid falling through any more shadows. At least his hands weren't disappearing like yesterday. Maybe that was a side effect of too much time spent in the shadow world before X'era rescued him.

Clenching his jaw, he pressed his palms into the flour against the dough. Flipping it, he pushed his palms into the sticky mixture in long threading motions. While he worked, he tracked the auditors. Right after one passed, he tore a coin-sized piece off and dropped it into a metal plate on a shelf near his knees and nudged it toward the next worker. They did the same and on and on it made its way down the line. The person at the end would stash it away and they'd give it to one of the worker's families. As long as the weight was nearly the same on the loaves, the auditors didn't notice if scraps went missing, but scraps added up.

Satisfied with the softness of the dough, he raised his hand. The auditor weighed the loaf, made a chalky checkmark on her tablet, and set another loaf before him. The kneaded dough was carted toward the rising room.

Putting all his strength into it, he kneaded as best he could, like his mother had shown him. It was one of the things his parents had agreed on before his Pa disappeared. Survival skills were essential. Of course, his father wanted him to use the skills for spying while his mother wanted him to use them for starting a family. His Pa had won out, and after his Pa disappeared—the spy began spying for the High Seers. The herbed dough clung to his fingers, smelling of home. He swallowed as loneliness threatened to drown him.

Raising his hand, he called for another loaf, and an auditor once again weighed his dough before providing him another. The spy's back burned as he continued at one and a half times the minimum production. He had to make it up to them all. Every fourth loaf, he gave the auditor the name of an absent coworker, or one who'd fallen behind, to give them credit for his labor. The auditors grunted, but they turned a blind eye as long as the daily quotas were met.

The smidge of shade on the spy's portion of the table turned inky.

"No," he hissed, reaching for the dough just as it fell through a shadow.

He blinked, glancing around. No one reacted. Hoping the job's monotony would keep anyone from noticing his missing hand, he pushed his hand through the darkest part of the darkness and noticed his hand pop out of a wall across the room. He patted around, feeling for the dough.

"Come here, you rat-sniffing—"

"Is everything alright?" An auditor shielded his eyes and frowned.

His fingers touching dough, he tugged it through the portal and started kneading, pretending he'd never stopped.

"Yes, fine," he said brightly, as Feng might.

The auditor squinted but continued meandering down the tables.

Sighing in relief, the spy kneaded the rest of his long shift. X'era's ring might keep him from falling between all the worlds, but he was going to get himself killed if he couldn't figure out his shadow magic in this one. He'd figured out that only the inky swirling shadows that audibly crackled were dangerous. They took on a strange sheen right before they opened between worlds. Interestingly, no one else seemed to have the issue of falling through. Something about that first shadow-step had given him this new ability. He'd have to practice later.

By the end of the workday, his shoulders and back were stiff. He wouldn't even have to pretend to hunch if he needed an elder costume in that moment. On the way out, he searched for Jun but couldn't located his friend in the throng of tired bakers.

Friend? The spy stopped. He never thought of anyone as his friend. Swallowing, he knew that he was displaying signs he'd been undercover too long. Only time off and away would resolve the matter. Once he delayed the invasion, he needed to leave, or he might make a fatal mistake.

He rolled out his shoulders, preparing for the rest of his long day. He had research to do on the Mooncursed while the sun was out and then reconnaissance tonight to determine how to keep the emperor from invading Avyllon. He'd sent the High Seer a warning and hoped she'd get it in time, but, either way, it was up to him to stall. And he did need a little sleep before tomorrow's shift, where he'd be assigned to the hot, damp rising room ovens all day. After washing the flour from his skin and changing out of his uniform, he headed to the library to begin his search.

At the library, he skimmed through a few books on wolves in the naturalist section. All other references of Mooncursed, except for a few old fairytales, had been removed. He flipped through a book titled "On Wolves," by Li Huang. Huang had spent most of the time discussing the evolution of wolves and predation patterns. Whatever that meant. And this thing was *so* old, dated five hundred years ago. He stopped flipping when his eyes caught on one section.

Centuries-old oral traditions of hereditary shapeshifting wolves, known as Lycanthrope, are found across Lythea. Werewolves, however, were said to be cursed by the moon when hunters murdered her favorite child, the wolf, and can infect others with scratch or bite. Both tales predate the emergence of the Mooncursed, which are Shadow-corrupted creatures. Neither man nor beast, they are akin to demons.

He closed the book, shaking his head.

Werewolves.

Lycanthrope.

Mooncursed.

There were different types? Head spinning, he set it back on the shelf and started skimming through another book. Glancing up, he noticed a familiar-looking woman chatting with a librarian. She chuckled and angled her face slightly toward him.

Quickly, he backed around a corner, sidling behind a tall stack of books. He buried his nose into the book, hiding his face.

It's the woman from the emperor's bedroom.

He peered through an empty section of books toward the tables she'd been standing next to, but she was gone. Hopefully she'd left. Turning to creep toward the exit, the book in his hands thudded into someone.

"Sorry," he mumbled.

The woman stood before him, and he knew a satisfied grin would split her face before it sank into her features. Her black hair was shorn at her shoulders and her amber eyes sparkled with delight as her muscles tensed in anticipation. Seconds later, triumph replaced delight and her posture settled as though she didn't expect him to run.

He puffed up his chest, raised up on the balls of his feet to increase his height, and leaned forward against the stack with a roving gaze. "Hello beautiful. The gods must be smiling upon me today. Do you want to go grab some wine and see where the day takes us? I have nowhere else to be." He cocked his eyebrow suggestively.

Her smug grin never left her lips as she raised her hands and proceeded to parrot back the series of hand gestures that he'd made at her the other night. And she'd taken some creative liberties with number five.

He couldn't help the amused twitch plaguing the corners of his mouth. Her eyes lit up as she glanced at his tell. She *definitely* recognized him. He fought to stay in character, out of habit.

He grinned. "I'm up to try any of those. You just tell me which one you want to start with. That fifth one..."

"You can drop the act. I know it's you." She crossed her arms. "Deny it and I'll yell for the guards."

His plastered-on smile faded as he leaned back. Stuffing his hands into his pockets, he set his heels on the ground and un-puffed his chest.

"What do you want?" he asked tightly.

"We need to talk. Let's go somewhere quieter," she said.

Ordinarily, he would have already vanished into the stacks, but he hesitated. He still needed help to accomplish his plans in time. If she was a rebel, she might have information about the Mooncursed and the army's whereabouts he could use, and then he could finally leave. He assumed the persona she would be expecting.

"I don't have a lot of time," he muttered, feigning disinterest to entice her to chase.

"This won't take long."

She turned on her heel and floated out of the library. Gods and goddesses, this felt like such a bad idea, but he could use the help, and their interests did seem aligned. He told himself it wasn't the spy-sickness or the fact that she was beautiful, cunning, and determined that pushed him to follow her outside when his instincts warned him otherwise. Setting down the book on the wrong shelf, he followed her out while avoiding all shadows with even a hint of gleam.

She led him to a small tea shop a few streets over. The owner poured them each a steaming cup of tea in delicate porcelain teacups and left them alone.

They both started talking at the same time.

"I've been looking—"

"What do you—"

He stopped and gestured for her to continue.

"I've been looking for you for three days."

He cradled the tea, grumbling. "People have searched for years and never found me."

"They questioned me for hours."

"I know."

"You waited for me to get released." She sipped the tea.

He hesitated, remembering what came next. "I did."

"I saw you. One moment you were there and the next moment you vanished into thin air. And that wasn't some spy trick. You literally fell through the ground and were gone."

He sipped tea as the hair on his neck prickled with danger.

"Who are you?" she pressed.

Dabbing his mouth with a small handkerchief, he studied her. He had a hundred aliases he could give her, but he didn't want to share any of them. Perhaps he'd share just a sliver of truth; it might help assuage his loneliness.

"I don't have a name," he said.

"Lie."

His brow lifted. "It's not a lie, entirely. True spies—" He added the next bit to maintain his current cover. "—or thieves do not use their name. They remain nameless so they're harder to catch. I do not use my name, so I do not have a name to share."

"Oh. I didn't know that."

"You're not a spy or a thief."

A crystal laugh rang out. "I got into that bedroom same as you and found you. Give me some credit."

"You could be a good spy."

She looked taken aback at first, but a small smile spread across her mouth and crinkled the edges of her eyes in a way he couldn't stop staring at. While he hid his every thought, she wore hers plainly, and it was as refreshing as lotus water.

She said, "I think you mean that as a compliment, so I'll take it."

"What's your name?"

"Mei."

He grinned into his teacup.

As if realizing that by sharing her name, she was admitting to being a poor spy, she stammered, "I need to know what you want though. What is your mission? You burned the map, so I don't believe you *only* wanted to steal it. There's something else."

He tapped his finger on the edge of the cup. Weighing how much truth to give her, he knew he couldn't stop an invasion on his own. He'd known that the night he'd fallen into the shadow she might be able to help but he couldn't tell her everything, no matter how much he yearned to.

"I don't want the emperor to grow any more powerful. I don't want him to invade Teridar. I don't want him to be emperor any longer," he said truthfully.

Her expression twisted. "Why?"

"My business."

"Just like how you disappeared is your business? Who do you spy for?"

He shrugged. "Whoever pays me to steal things or find things."

She squinted. "Are you a spy or a thief then?"

He said nothing.

"We could have used that map," she grumbled.

"Whatever you wanted it for, he wanted it for much worse. Better for no one to have it."

She groaned and continued, "I think we want the same thing. I think we can help each other. We want to overthrow him."

"Why?"

"Because he's a conquering tyrant who is terrorizing the city. He promises food and shelter for all, but we've seen none of it. Things are just as bad as before except now people are afraid with good reason."

"That we agree on," the spy said.

Her motivations were straightforward enough. Her face betrayed her every thought, and he had no reason to doubt her words. Deception had long been his constant companion, and he sensed none from her. She'd found someone who could help her get close to the emperor and wanted to bring him into the fold. It all checked out.

He tilted his head, having no love lost for the people who'd killed his grandmother and nearly killed his father all those years ago. "If overthrowing him stops him from invading, I'll help."

"You'd help us overthrow him?"

"I intend to burn every single effigy of his false goddess as well." The heat in his words surprised him; he must have taken X'era's anger as his own.

Her brows rose. They sipped tea in silence for a few moments. It tasted of lotus berry and honey with hints of smoke. His chest filled with hope. It sounded like they might very well have the information he sought, making this risk worth taking.

"The emperor is moving his army to the isthmus tomorrow. I know someone whose cousin wrote and said they'd be leaving for a while," she said.

His adrenaline spiked. "Just to the isthmus? Or into Avyllon?"

"Not into Avyllon yet."

He's still looking for the monuments or artifacts. Burning the map protected the locations. It had worked.

"What're you going to do?" she asked.

"What do you know of the Mooncursed 'shrine'," the spy answered.

"Mooncursed?"

"If you haven't seen them yet, you probably will. They're magically created monsters."

"Ah." She chewed her lip. "I'll let our network know to hide old maps and see if they've heard of the 'shrine.'"

"Thank you."

She slipped a small scrap of paper toward him. "This is how to contact me."

The spy watched her leave the tea house and easily melt into the crowed in a way that was precise as a scalpel and poetic as a song. He smiled to himself. While he'd never been one for partners, it wouldn't be the worst thing to have to work with her for a little while.

Leaving minutes later, he returned to his apartment. He had some spying to do and not much time to do it. And before that, he had to get a handle on his new magic or Avyllon would perish.

SHADOWSTEPPING
CHAPTER SEVEN

Shadowstepping was both simpler and more difficult than anything the nameless one had ever done. And he'd cracked vaults, infiltrated palaces, escaped dungeons, and become the goat whisperer of a small village in rural Arryn for a few months. He'd trained a half dozen goats to attack visitors and bring him only mildly chewed vegetables from the garden while he hid out and cracked a difficult code. No, shadowstepping was the thing that might undo him. He'd fallen through several dozen shadows that afternoon and was no closer to navigating his new abilities than when he started. He slowly pulled himself off the floorboards, rubbing his backside.

I don't get it.

Sometimes, he made it into the shadow world, and other times he was dropped onto his head through a random nearby shadow. But what changed? He glanced at the darkest two shadows in the room—both swirling and telling him they'd serve as a portal. One skill he'd picked up was that he could locate them easily now. He just couldn't control where they spit him out.

How had he done it that first night when he'd fallen through all those worlds? He remembered feeling disoriented, detached, and strange. If he replicated that feeling, maybe it would help.

He stilled, searching for the feeling from that night. Heartbeat slowing as his mind emptied, he willed himself to be unseen as he had so many missions before. A chill settled on his skin as he imagined himself drawing in all the darkness from the room. Sound trickled away. Eyes half-lidded, he stepped into the inky, gleaming shadow beside his small copper bathing tub.

Holding onto the feeling, he walked through the shifting phantom walls of the apartments. A laughing pair of women doted on several young children. The family was barely whispers, outlines, like partially finished illustrations moving and jumping through space. They didn't seem to notice him as he slipped through the walls.

Shining slivers of light where shadow portals would be in the other world blinked at him, letting him see back into reality. He floated through the wall and down to the street—full of wispy outlines of people. The shadow world twisted and fogged, preparing to toss him out again. He fought to maintain the serene quiet feeling from his missions, finding that formless sensation.

Pain burned his fingertips, originating from his bones. It spread up one arm, lancing into the bones in his shoulder. His body fought the shadows. He pushed off the red cobblestones and floated back toward his third-level apartment. Passing a window, a beaming child waved to him. He waved back just as his fingers crackled with searing agony. He clawed through his wall toward a bright, white sliver.

Warm, sticky heat pooled around him as he returned to the world of mortals. He took a deep breath, shielding his eyes against the light. His hand flickered in and out, solid to smoke and back.

Breathe. Focus. Stay on mission.

Wiggling his burning fingers, he began to count. Seven minutes. Longer than last time. He exhaled. It was a start. He'd figured out how to reach the shadow world. It'd have to be good enough for tonight because he had work to do.

The first task was breaking into the imperial military offices and stealing an army.

Casting wary glances at any too-dark shadows nearby, the spy crouched on a rooftop across from the imperial military office. Mei dropped down beside him, wearing all black and gray from head to toe.

"I was surprised to hear from you," she whispered.

"They're moving the troops today. It's our only chance. Did you find the maps?"

She adjusted the mask over her nose and mouth. "Yes. There were only a few that were that old, but we spread word to hide the maps or references to monuments. He won't find them."

"Did you learn anything about the shrine?"

"There are only a few places it could be. The guards and wardens keep that to themselves. But there are a few temples big enough for the type of thing you described."

"Thanks."

Her eyes crinkled, showing she was smiling under the mask. "What's the plan?"

"I was thinking about it all day while I was..." He stopped.

"Being secretive."

He grinned despite himself, finding it hard to look away from her. "Sure. Being secretive. If I want to keep the emperor from invading, I need to move his army farther away. It'll send things into chaos and give Teridar time to prepare. Then I'll figure out what to do from there."

"You're just going to move his army? How?"

"Smaller towns are the hardest to infiltrate. Everyone knows everyone. Everyone talks. The larger you get, the more people rely on administrative logs, letters, records, and the like. They don't even stop to question when a seven is turned into an eight, or when they receive an order to move the army across the continent. Even if they weren't expecting it."

"And Demorra is the biggest empire in the world."

He nodded. "In some ways the easiest to work within. I just need a single piece of imperial letterhead and the emperor's seal."

"What do you need me to do?"

"Did you get what I asked for?"

"The imperial messenger uniform?" She patted her satchel. "I have to return it tomorrow or it'll be noticed."

"And the nametag?"

"Got it too." She grinned.

"Good. Put it on. I'll get the seal and the parchment after they've locked up. I'll write the order, but we'll be cutting it close to when they leave for the day, so you need to be in uniform and ready to deliver it. Run up just as the office is closing and hand them this. You'll have to be convincing."

She tugged the uniform from her satchel and wrangled it over her dark clothes. He grinned. He didn't even have to tell her to layer disguises. She was a natural.

Smoothing the uniform, she asked, "Are you going to teach me your trick where you disappear into thin air?"

Shadowstepping could very well cost a person their body and soul. Even if he knew how to share this magic, he'd be hesitant to sentence anyone else to this.

"We'll see," he hedged.

He stilled his mind, searching for the feeling of disappearing. The shadows gleamed all around him, even those that should have been too faint to step through.

"Meet you around front in a few minutes."

As she peered toward their target, he stepped through a shadow behind her and was gone.

The spy floated down to the street before walking through a wall. He darted through offices, searching for the one that controlled troop movements. Squinting, he tried to read the letters on the desks, to see which officer sent the orders. Finally, he found it.

Checking the hall to ensure it was empty, he stepped through the shadow and reached for a blank stamped page. His hand slipped through the table. He cursed, reaching with his other hand, but both had flickered out of existence. He'd stayed in the other world too long. He began to count.

Voices echoed in the hall along with boot steps. Three minutes. He reached for the paper, but his hand was still formless. The door handle jingled. His blood rushed. He leaned down and bit the paper before lunging into a shadow. The door opened just as he slipped into the other world.

Carefully taking the paper from his mouth, he waited in the shadow world. The officer plopped down in the padded leather chair and put his feet up before lighting a pipe. He wasn't going anywhere anytime soon. The chair was too close to the drawers that likely held the seal of his office.

The spy needed a distraction, and he'd suspected he might, which was why he'd asked Mei to come. He floated back up to the rooftop where Mei was patting the roof tiles, searching for how he'd accomplished his trick. He stepped out of a shadow behind her and tapped her back. She whirled on him, drawing a small dagger. Her feline expression softened.

"How'd you do it!" she whispered.

He lifted the paper. "I need a seal but got interrupted. I need a distraction so I can open the drawer and get the seal out."

"How long do you need?"

"Five minutes to write the order, heat the wax, and get the seal back."

She nodded and tiptoed off the roof. He slipped back into the shadow world and returned to the office.

A knock sounded on the door. "What is it?" the officer snapped.

"Sir, there are several fires reported in all the surrounding neighborhoods."

Fires? She really was a quick study. He chuckled.

The man's boots hit the floor. "Send guards."

The door closed as the officer followed the guard out. The spy stepped out of a shadow and quickly searched for the seal.

"Got it," he murmured.

He found an imperial order and copied the language. He scrawled the ink in matching patterns and terms, changing only the destination. All troops would be immediately sent to Ala'end to quell an uprising.

The other end of the continent, far from Avyllon.

Too easy.

He took the heated wax and was about to seal the document until he noticed the broken seal on the other. Hesitating, he put down the wax and carefully lined the broken edges of the seal up. A howling wolf crest in a moon.

The emperor's personal seal.

Not the officer's seal. He cursed. He hadn't counted on the emperor personally signing every troop movement order. There was no way he'd get to the palace and back. If he could even find the seal. But he had an idea. Maybe it could work. He heated a letter opener and carefully slid the hot metal underneath the emperor's seal to free it from the letter. He dribbled a few drops of hot wax onto his document and attached the old broken seal.

It'd have to do.

He dumped out the rest of the wax and slid the seal into the drawer and the doorknob turned.

Locating the gleaming shadow behind the door, he stepped inside as the door opened.

"Savages! Who would burn goat excrement in Niamh's offering bowls? This recreant must be found," the officer hissed.

The spy chuckled as he slipped through the walls and back outside. Mei was chaos in human form. He loved it. It was the opposite of his approach, but he could easily slip through the confusion.

Mei waited at the front door, pretending to smoke a pipe. He slipped the letter into the crook of her arm.

"The seal is broken," he whispered. "You need to break it on accident when you deliver it. I hope your acting skills are brushed off."

She jumped, glancing around before noticing the letter in her arm.

"Where are you? You've gotta teach me," she hissed the wrong direction.

Straightening her stolen uniform, she strode toward the guards at the front door. "I have an urgent missive from the emperor."

Pretending to slip, she made a show of crushing the letter on the ground beneath her palm and cursing. Standing, she shook her head at the sight of the cracked seal.

"The emperor is going to flay me for this," she said.

The guard hesitated. "I'll tell the administrator I watched the seal crack. Come this way."

Feeling his half-corporeal body begin to burn, the nameless one left the shadow world and hugged a corner across the street.

A few minutes later, Mei walked out of the administration office beaming. He waved and she walked toward him.

"They bought it! The troops are going."

"Let's get out of here before they see us," he said, a smile cracking his face.

He darted down the road and she raced behind him. As dawn approached, the city streets began filling will people either heading to work or taking up their daily chores. In this part of the city, the buildings were half-crumbling and hastily repaired with a patchwork of mortar, straw, and prayers. Coppers, not gold, exchanged hands, and more often than not the bartering was with goods and not coin at all. The busy neighborhood housed generations of families and had expanded by several rows of shoddy buildings recently to include new warehouse workers.

Standing outside his apartment, he realized that he'd foolishly led her back here. How had it not occurred to him to go elsewhere? The spy-sickness was becoming a liability. Her eyes glimmered with the excitement of a successful mission, and her cheeks were flush. She shifted her weight from foot to foot as if ready to go do another. He allowed himself a grin, knowing all too well the draw toward this work.

Voices cut through their thrill, and both their heads snapped toward the scene unfolding. Three imperial guards surrounded an old man wearing a threadbare apron outside of a straw and mud house.

"You've been warned already. This is your third warning. The offering bowl has remained empty for a week," an imperial guard snapped.

"I don't recognize Niamh. My loyalty is to Zaehala alone." The elderly man struggled against the grips of guards.

The spy pressed against the wall beside Mei, willing them both to be invisible in the too-narrow streets. An inky shadow reached for him —offering him refuge but he couldn't leave her again.

The imperial guard's face twisted. Quietly, she said, "You don't want to say that. You know the penalty for defying Niamh."

The nameless one wanted to shout to the man to take it back. He couldn't imagine the gods faulting the man for a few honeyed words when actions mattered more. Lie. Drop a few scraps into the purple offering bowl. But not this...

The man wrenched his arm from the guards' grip, bruises already forming on his papery skin. "I know the penalty, but I won't lie and worship a false goddess."

A collective gasp emerged from the gathering crowd.

The spy's heart fell. He knew what the old man felt. He'd never recognize Niamh after X'era's words. The terror he'd felt when she snarled at the worship of Niamh rattled his bones.

"Let go of me," the old man demanded, struggling against ashen imperial guards.

"He's just an old man." The spy heard words spilling from his lips, in his voice, before he'd realized what he'd done. "Here, I'll pay his offering. He doesn't know what he's saying. He's just confused." The spy dropped several coins, a generous offering, into the man's bowl.

The imperial guards glanced to their captain. She hesitated, regarding the spy and the elderly man. Her mouth was set into a thin line, and by the twitch of her lips, she hated this.

"Let him go," she finally said.

Relief flooded the spy. He stepped back toward the wall beside Mei, letting the shadows drag attention from them. There was some morality left here. These were good people fighting impossible circumstances. But if they had the right choice, it seemed they'd make it.

"Arrest him!" a new voice cracked.

A warden in full titan ore armor pushed through the crowd. Yellow eyes glowed from within the helm. His limbs were too long, bent at the wrong places. A tuft of fur peeked out from the top of his boots.

Oh, hells.

The spy realized why the wardens looked so strange. Images of that cursed incinerator flooded his brain. They were experiments, not so different from the Mooncursed. Humans enhanced with corrupted magic.

The guards hesitantly grabbed the old man again.

"I won't recognize Niamh." The old man damned himself.

The warden kicked the old man's legs with a loud crunch, and the man fell to his knees.

"Then die."

The warden drew his thin, curved sword and cut off the man's head. In the middle of the road. With people around. With children around. The spy's brain whirlpooled into a paralyzed churning mass.

The man's body slumped to the ground. The imperial guards gaped. People screamed and darted inside open doorways. Blood trickled through the ruddy cobblestones.

"Everyone get inside or get to your work assignments now," the warden commanded. "We'll be checking all offering bowls."

The spy stared, his mind fighting to accept the horrors, but dragged Mei toward his apartment. Little choice remained but to reveal the location of his home.

Inside, she blinked back tears. "I can't believe they killed him."

His heart ached for her.

Gods—it was stupid. But he reached out and hugged her. Knowing she needed a modicum of comfort after the thrill and then murder. Not everyone could compartmentalize as he could, as he'd been raised to do. He squeezed her shoulders as they peered out the window at the scene below.

Lifting his bloody katana, the warden plopped the head into the offering bowl. "Remember this day. Defy Niamh and die."

Unlikely Partners
Chapter Eight

The spy hurried out of his apartment a half hour later, wrapping the apron around his hips. He grabbed Mei's hand and dragged her down the stairs behind him. He was already so late, and did not want to bring her here, but he needed to make sure to escort her out of that neighborhood while it was still crawling with wardens and guards.

"This is where you live?" she asked.

"What did you expect?" He flew down the stairs, hoping to not be the last one to check in to work.

"Like a bird nest on the top of one of the spires, or a cave where your disguises are displayed on mannequins like trophies. Or a stone cottage where you sleep upside down surrounded by coded letters."

He nearly tripped. "What? Where did you get those ideas?"

She shrugged. "I like to read."

"What sort of books have you been reading? Actually, don't tell me. I'm late for work."

"You have a *job*?" She gaped.

"Don't you?" He rolled his eyes. "I need food. It would look suspicious if I didn't work, and I can't just have bags of gold laying around."

"*Bags* of gold? How rich are you?" She followed him, jogging down the street toward the bakery. "Who do you work for?"

He snorted. "A spy never tells." He waggled his eyebrows over his shoulder. "Who do you work for?"

She grunted, tailing him until he caught the end of the workers filing into the bakery.

Thank X'era.

He wasn't late yet. Though he didn't need the job, he couldn't let Jun down again.

"I'll contact you later." He waved before following the stragglers inside.

He already knew his assignment for the day and hurried toward the rising rooms.

Jun's voice interrupted him. "How do you know Mei?"

The spy turned to see Jun claiming a workstation beside him. "I was helping her with something."

The lies danced from his tongue. He'd spent so much of his life lying, he hardly had to try.

Vague was good. Some truth helped sell it. Assume they know more than you think and let them talk more than you do. People will fill the silence if you let them. You just need to listen.

His father's teachings lived in his head.

Jun leaned forward. "Are you part of... Are you helping her with..."

The spy could guess what filled those gaps. She must have a reputation with the rebels. He nodded slowly.

Jun leaned back. "Is that why you were gone the other day?"

The spy accepted his first kneaded loaf from the auditor and dipped a rag in boiled water. He wrapped the rag around the edge of the loaf pan and placed it into an oven. He flipped an hourglass, setting the time for that oven.

He joined Jun again. "I got held up with some work."

"That's why your explanation was so terrible?" Jun asked.

The spy nearly chuckled and nodded. He worked on another loaf, preparing it to rise.

"Last night too," the spy said.

"I'm sorry I yelled at you," Jun murmured. "I should've known you wouldn't just leave us in a lurch like that. I was a bad friend to assume."

The spy smiled and continued their work. The shift passed more quickly than others had, and it wasn't until the end that the spy realized he hadn't had any shadow-related accidents. He should have been thrilled, but the old man's face before the warden's katana came down dampened his spirits.

Jun caught his arm outside the bakery. "I want to help. My children won't grow up in a place like this. Let me know what you need."

The spy nodded. He watched Jun walk the opposite direction. He hated to admit it, but there were people in Demorra worth helping. Once he was done helping the High Seer protect Avyllon, was he really going to be able to leave?

Mei perched on the extended windowsill of his apartment when he got home. Her legs dangled three stories above the streets below. He tugged the apron off and laid it across the wooden table in the kitchen before climbing out onto the narrow sill beside her. It was so narrow their legs touched as she kicked her feet. Her black hair was freed from the plaits he'd always seen it in.

"Your place is weird. It's not weird enough," she said.

He chuckled. "That's the point. If you don't look too closely, it's painfully ordinary." He pointed behind him. "My broom has a few wigs hidden inside. The disguise sewing materials are in the kitchen drawer. The blanket doubles as a cloak. My face paints and clays are hidden in the hearth in the ashes."

She studied each location he pointed out, squinting against the afternoon sun. "Hiding in plain sight."

"Blending in is about fitting in," he said. "Knowing how to belong but to settle into the waves of human behavior. There are patterns if you look for them. You want people to *feel* as though you belong, you've always belonged, you've been there forever. But they're not able to recall your face or name the next day."

"That sounds incredibly lonely," she said.

His gut twisted. Aurienne hadn't intended to send him on another job after being abroad so long, but the emperor's missive had forced her hand. And working with Mei definitely had helped.

"It can be. Family helps. Friends help." He glanced at her, deciding to tell her something entirely real. "I visit my mother for a while between every mission. I stay for days or weeks in that little town. They think I'm a merchant, so my absences aren't missed. But every time I see her, it grounds me. I remember who I am behind the names and faces I shed."

She chewed her lip. "What about partners?"

He'd usually worked alone unless a particular mission demanded it, but a partner? Never. He glanced at the sprawling city, thinking of all the people within. He couldn't do this alone, not in time.

And she'd helped, held her own. Thought on her feet. Never betrayed his secrets. And she'd found him within days. She'd be a good partner, at least for a while. She was a rebel, a fighter, and didn't need to be reminded of the risks. She knew what she was asking.

"A partner would be nice, too."

"Great." She beamed. "Now teach me the trick where you disappear."

He threw his head back and laughed loudly for a few seconds before wiping his eyes. Not all his secrets could be given so freely. And her joining him in rebel-spy activities was one thing. He wasn't sure his conscience would allow him to open her eyes to the shadow world—even if he knew how.

An inky shadow winked at him from behind his curtains. The best stories were vague and part truth. He reached his hand into the shadow, into the shadow world and it disappeared.

"You expect to see nothing, so you don't." He brought his hand back into their world.

"It was really gone!" She leaned back and put her hand into the shadow and wiggled her fingers.

Unlike his hand, hers remained visible.

He covered her hand with his and pressed it into the inky spot he knew she couldn't see. Her fingers disappeared underneath his.

"Whoa," she murmured.

He pulled their hands back into the sun, skin tingling where they touched. "It's just about feeling invisible."

Her brows furrowed as she focused intently, and he was drawn to her eyes rather than her hand. They were so close, and he found himself studying every detail. She stilled and slowly, ever so slowly, she dipped her fingers into the shadows, and they disappeared.

Did she just...

The outlines of her fingers appeared again, and she beamed. He blinked, shaking his head.

No. Just his imagination—becoming invisible as he had so many times before the magic. It couldn't be the magic.

"Look," he pointed to the golden road in the distance leading away from the city.

The golden road spanned the length of the continent, connecting all the great cities. It wove through the mountains, now full of army regiments leading away. If he could see it—the palace could.

"We did that," she breathed.

Allowing, himself a rare moment of satisfaction, he cocked a brow at his new partner. "We did."

He leaned against the window; it was time to get some answers from the rebels. "What have *you* learned?"

"The rebels have hidden all the maps of Teridar they could find," she said. "They're still locating and hiding them as we speak. They've also located the shrine."

His blood spiked. The gamble to work with the rebels had already paid off. She toed the floorboards, and he stiffened. Of course, there was a catch.

"They have a trade," she said. "There's a hostage they want released in exchange for the information."

"Who?"

"A political adversary from the region of Wolf Run that he locked up. One who's powerful and could aid our cause."

Not like he had a choice.

"Fine," he sighed. "Where?"

"The royal dungeons." Her wide smile was apologetic and slightly excited.

He rubbed his temples. That was going to be a problem. Prior to infiltrating the throne room, he'd investigated the dungeons and found it was nearly impossible to get in or out. Part of his goal was to find a way out if he was captured, and he'd found none from the inside. Getting someone out was theoretically possible if luck was on their side and he could control his magic well enough. Both were questionable, but he needed to know where the shrine was so he could sabotage the Mooncursed.

He cracked his knuckles. "What do you say we free a prisoner?"

DUNGEONS
CHAPTER NINE

Not a single shadow turned inky and shimmering around the palace or Niamh's temples. The spy circled them both, searching for any he could slip through, but something guarded the perimeter. The spy ate an apple, glancing at the black metal bars with diamond and gold flecks atop the high walls. Titan ore—on the windows and decorative elements on the walls too.

"Where are they finding all this titan ore?" he murmured to Mei.

"It's coming in on ships. They take workers out for three months at a time to mines, and bring back the ore," she said.

The rebels were as well-informed as he'd hoped.

He squinted. "Three months at a time? How much ore comes back?"

"I have no idea, but I have heard the miners say that they're going to the hells. They have to pay them high wages to get anyone to agree."

Hells? Like they're near the Nyx'ela mountains? Said to be the realm of the gods, the Nyx'ela mountain range was rumored to have a gleaming city high in the peaks. The stories also said that doorways to the hells opened, and if the miners said they were going to the hells, they could mean those mountains where dark beasts emerged from the hellish doorways and prowled the mist.

A piece of apple fell from his mouth.

Portals to the hells.

Just like the shadows he was stepping through. Maybe there was more truth to those legends than he realized. How many other stories were true?

Returning to the present matter, he allowed his gaze to wander over the palace. The iron front gates were forged to look like snarling dragons, and yellow stones reflected the sun in their eyes and mouths. Red curved tiles covered the flat rooftops many stories above the ground. The reddish walls were nearly sheer, save for hundreds upon hundreds of windows and balconies. Guards on horses patrolled in groups of six, leaving no entry point at the front.

While the nearby temple, covered in crushed purple crystals, remained outside the high gates and stone walls, it was just as impenetrable. There was a single entrance unless a person was willing to climb through the attic as he'd done several weeks ago when he discovered remnants of magical experiments gone wrong.

"How do we get in?" she whispered.

He'd been planning to sneak in through the shadows, but there were no portals. Later, he'd have to figure out why, but for now they'd make do.

"The old-fashioned way." He grinned when she quirked a brow.

The spy pushed off the wall and tossed the apple into one of the many smoldering fire pits illuminating the roads outside the palace. He bent down, flipping his cloak with an easy motion. When he stood, he wore a royal gardener's green cloak. It happened to be an Avyllon gardener's cloak, but it was close enough to avoid suspicion from a distance.

Mei's mouth dropped open. "But you... that cloak is black on one side and gray on the other. How is it green?"

He grinned, not ready to part with all his secrets. "Let's go."

The spy navigated the crowd until he reached the quieter street beside the imperial gardens. He waited until the street was clear and pushed through a thorny hedge.

The thorns caught on his cloak, tearing his skin and leaving thin lines of blood. He pushed slowly in, carefully leaning this way and that to deflect the thorns. Each cut stung, forcing him to call on his training to force the pain away.

"This is. Possibly. The worst way in. Ever." Mei hissed every word. She yelped, and then yelped again.

"Don't fight the thorns, just to imagine them brushing by you," he muttered back.

Once his head was freed from the hedge, he glanced around. The gardens were empty. A fountain bubbled between the rosebushes and lotus plants. Stepping out, he picked the thorns from his skin as he inspected himself. He was bleeding in a dozen places, but his thick cloak was mostly intact, and they'd gotten in much quicker than he'd expected.

"Not bad," he said.

"*Not bad*?" Mei panted as she finally exited the hedge in a crumpled puddle.

"The sewers are just as likely to drown you as let you through." He pulled a thorn out of his neck with a hiss. "Climbing isn't possible in daylight, and a single misplaced step can send you falling to your death. Walking in the front door is only possible with weeks of planning and set up. You can try to hide in an incoming cart, but if they find you, you're dead. This is about as good an entry as you can get."

She tugged thorns out of her legs and arms, wincing and muttering. When he started meandering toward the palace, stopping at random florae as a gardener would, she stumbled after him holding a dented watering can. The orderly garden maze stretched for several square miles in each direction behind the palace.

They reached the side entry to the gold and red palace, and he paused. Pretending to prune a nearby hedge, he waited for the guards to pass. The hooves of the horses clicked on the cobblestones as the guards patrolled by, but the two commonplace gardeners watering hedges attracted no attention.

After they passed, the spy pointed to the series of wide doors on the side of the building across the wide stone road. A never-ending cloud of steam escaped the doors, smelling of lye and bleach. Rows of drying racks bending under the weight of the linens were nestled between the two buildings.

"The laundry is that way, and we need a distraction. We need two uniforms that won't be missed or noticed for a while to keep the count off for a while." At her confused expression, he added, "Getting out without anyone knowing you were there is just as important as getting in. Especially if you aren't immediately leaving the country. Now can you handle the distraction? I'll get the uniforms."

"Won't they know we're in the wrong clothes if they see us wearing this?" She pulled at her clothes.

"Yes."

"Okay." A devious grin tugged at the corners of her mouth. "You stay out of sight; I'll create a distraction."

The spy slipped into the back of the laundry, behind the carts of soiled linens. Square cut pools of various dyes, soaps, and rinse water filled the room. Laundresses walked on thin paths between the pools. Along one wall, bottles of various brightly colored liquids formed neat lines.

Lying flat, he peered out from underneath the cart, excited to see what Mei would come up with. Her chaos was intoxicating for someone as disciplined as him.

Before he knew it, Mei was swathed in a long curtain and a few odd pieces of bedding, stumbling and screaming.

"Help!" she screamed, before she went headfirst into one of the frothy rinse water pools.

Several dozen laundresses started shouting at once. The water churned as the women pulled their stout stirring poles from the steaming water.

"Help her!"

"Someone help!"

"She could drown."

Mei broke the water's surface, half draped in the curtain, and wearing a maid's uniform. She'd somehow gotten a uniform over her head and on while under the water. His brows rose. That took extraordinary skill—especially with no planning. She had the makings of a master spy.

He shook his head and took advantage of the chaos to search for a uniform and grimaced at what he found. Only maids' uniforms were nearby. He snatched one and tugged it on. He stuffed an extra uniform under his shirt for the prisoner.

A laundress pulled a dripping, crying Mei from the water. "I'm so sorry. The emperor's chamber steward sent me here with soiled linens from some accident and said to come back as quickly as I could, and I tripped—"

The spy hastily tied on the uniform and clasped a few buttons while attention was on Mei. It was a brilliant plan. No one could see what she was wearing when she went into the pool, and she came out in a uniform. No one would question whether she belonged. This partnership might work out after all.

"Quickly, get her a dry uniform," one of the laundresses ordered.

Minutes later, Mei was laden with linens and sent on her way. The spy snatched a soapy cleaning bucket and rag from the corner before following her out. They passed pairs of guards at every corner whose hawkish gazes missed little.

"Impressive," he whispered as his long strides took him ahead of her.

Holding tall stacks of folded linens that obscured her face, Mei followed the spy down the corridor.

"You pull off that maid uniform," Mei snickered.

The spy rolled his eyes, taking measured steps toward the private chambers. There were twice as many guards in this corridor since the botched map heist turned arson incident. The guards hardly looked at the spy, who walked the center of the hall with his head down.

"How do you do it? People barely look at you," she whispered.

"Convince yourself you belong, and act like it," he said.

"Godsdamned advice makes no sense," she muttered.

The back corridors of the palace lacked the gilded ornamentation of the living and meeting rooms. Tapestries and dragon sculptures gave way to plain, smooth redstone walls. Rounding the corner, he found the barred doorway leading to the basements. Six burly guards with shaved heads and single top knot of hair were posted outside.

"Shh. The entrance to the dungeons is right there," the spy said.

"Halt." A guard stopped them just outside the door.

The spy kept his head down, respectfully, and painted on a neutral expression. He adopted a high-pitched trill of a maid. "We were asked to clean up after the prisoner."

The spy tapped the bucket as proof, and Mei held out the linens.

"I didn't hear anything about that," the guard scowled.

Another guard held up his knobby hand. "We can't let you in without approval."

The spy offered the guard his bucket and tried to look eager to hand it off. "I understand. You will have to take it down though. The water is to help with the prisoner's smell, and the bucket will swap with the prisoner's overflowing personal relief bucket."

Keeping his head down under the maid's cap, he held up the bucket, soapy water sloshing over the edges. It was the riskiest part of the mission. If the guards suspected they were too eager, they'd question them. He tried to breathe slowly instead of holding his breath.

"What're the linens for?" a guard asked.

"The *accident*," Mei said quietly, looking away. "The relief bucket hadn't been changed quickly enough and the prisoner became upset. It's apparently all over the cell, so they sent me with all this. Between that and the interrogation injuries, the mess is considerable."

The spy almost grinned.

The guard's eyes widened slightly as his nostrils flare in disgust at the implication. He glanced down the hall and back at the spy. Then he glanced at the other five guards at the door. One shrugged. The others stared straight forward—refusing to take part in this.

"I haven't heard about any accident—" the guard with two yellow, cracked teeth started.

The captain held up a clinking ring of rusted keys. "Just handle it."

The spy bowed and nodded as he brought down the bucket. "As you say."

He unlocked the door, and Mei and he entered the top of the stairwell to the dungeons. The door closed behind them with a bang, leaving them to stare at the dark path before them. Flickering torches barely illuminated their path.

X'era's blessings.

It worked. This was the most half-baked plan he'd ever undertaken. And yet—he was already having more fun than he'd remembered. When had a job last been any fun?

Glancing at Mei, he noticed she was pale, breathing hard, but her eyes shone with excitement. The linens shook in her hands.

"Easy, easy," he cautioned. "You don't want to be sick. It'll blow our cover. Take slow, measured breaths."

She nodded, breathing in and out slowly.

The spy led them down the stairs, blindly proceeding deeper into the dungeons without a clear layout. He'd never been able to obtain one before. At the bottom of the stairs, three guards were playing cards at a low table.

A guard stood. "What're you two doing down here?"

"We were told to bring these for the prisoner," the spy answered, holding up the keys.

"Which one?"

Mei opened her mouth, but the spy stepped in front of her. Having too much knowledge was suspicious. Knowing the name of the prisoner could be a sure sign that they had ulterior motives.

He replied coolly in the same high-pitched voice of a maid, "They didn't tell us any names. Or how many are here. Can you point us in the right direction?"

The guard made a harrumph sound in his throat.

"They said he was here a while?" Mei offered, glancing at the spy questioningly, apparently having gotten the hint.

"Down that way. He's the only one in that corridor." The guard waved his hand in the general direction and sat down at the card table.

Somehow their luck hadn't yet run out.

The spy and Mei walked down the row of cells, stopping at the third on the left. A guard was posted just outside the cell, leaning back and flipping through a leaflet. At their arrival, he stood and crossed his arms.

The guard said, "What're you doing here?"

"Here to clean up the cell?" the spy answered.

"It doesn't need cleaning." The guard chewed on dark, sticky lotus honey, lips smacking as he spoke.

It could all unravel here. They needed to get into the cell to free the prisoner, and this was the final obstacle. If he called the alarm, there would be no escaping the hordes of guards they'd passed on the way in, and there was no escape from this prison from the inside. The titan ore cell bars were too dense to cut through, and there was no way to tunnel through the monolithic stones the palace was built upon. The only way in or out was with a key.

"We just do what we're told, sir," Mei said demurely. "Should we leave the linens and bucket with you?"

The guard glanced from the pair to the cell and back. "Leave them here. I can't open the door without orders."

The tactic they'd used at the main door didn't work. They had to get the cell open, or this was all for nothing. Mei was looking to him, and the spy had only a few possible options—none of them good.

"You can go," the guard said tightly, hand drifting toward his katana.

The spy glanced toward the cell, where a human-shaped lump lied under a thin blanket on a cot.

"Of course," the spy bowed again, keeping his head down.

He set the bucket beside the guard's chair and backed away. Mei placed the tall stack of fresh linens beside it, shooting questioning looks toward the spy.

"Is there a problem?" the guard demanded.

The spy pretended to toy with the maid's apron. "Can we wait here until you verify our orders? If we leave this job unfinished, we could lose our jobs. They're very strict."

A few steps closer and he could incapacitate the soldier. He had to buy time because they wouldn't likely get this lucky again. This was his one shot to help the rebellion and learn the location of the shrine. And it was slipping through his fingers.

"I'll ensure it's finished." The guard backed up a few paces, drawing the katana a hand's width. "It's time for you to go."

The spy took a step forward, putting his hand up placatingly. "We'll go. But what is your name so we can let our bosses know that we left on your orders."

The guard opened his mouth wide—about to sound the alarm.

The spy was about to dart in, but he was too far away. They would be found out in just seconds. Mei's eyes widened, and she froze.

Thud.

The guard's eyes unfocused, and he fell forward, unconscious.

The prisoner was standing behind the guard, with his arm through the bars holding his wooden water cup. He pulled his hand back through the bars.

"I hope you are actually here to get me out and aren't just really enthusiastic about your jobs." The man grinned.

The spy lifted a brow at the man appreciatively. "Good timing.

Sliding the key into the titan ore lock, the spy gave it a hard turn. The door swung open.

"What's the plan?" The man started stripping the ragged clothing.

Mei paled, and she quickly turned around.

The spy removed the extra maid costume from under his shirt, but the man shook his head.

"I'll wear what he's wearing." The man nodded toward the guard's uniform.

The man picked up the bucket of water and dumped it over his head, quickly scrubbing away the blood and dirt from his face and hands. Then he began stripping the guard. After taking his weapon and clothes, he began putting them on.

Bending down, the spy redressed the guard in the man's discarded rags. He ripped the maid uniform into strips to bind the man's hands to his feet, and to gag him.

As he was about to drag the guard into the cell, the man approached. "I'm Jarron."

He held out his hand and the spy shook it. "I don't have a name."

"What they say about spies is true then?"

Mei glanced over her shoulder, frowning.

The two men dragged the guard into the cell, tying him to the bars, and draping the raggedy blanket over him.

"How're we getting out of here?" Jarron whispered, straightening the stolen uniform.

"Has to be the same way we got in," the spy replied.

Mei's eyes flashed. "We did promise them a mess."

Darting toward the refuse bucket, she flung it all over the wall and hallway. Collecting the moldy food from the prisoner's tray, she spread it across the floor. She tossed the linens over it, and the linens soaked it up. Cracking the replacement bucket she hurled broken boards in every direction. Then she knocked over the guard's stool.

"That'll keep them busy," she said.

The spy swallowed. "We're gonna need proof."

Cringing, Mei collected a dripping ball of linens.

Jarron grimaced. "That is vile."

"There are three guards playing cards," the spy explained. "Tell them the prisoner has gone mad. You subdued him but had to get us out of there because it was not safe. They need back up."

"Understood."

The spy glanced to Mei. "Are you ready to sell it?"

She was turning a sickly color of green but nodded firmly.

"Help!" Jarron stumbled toward the three guards around the corner, guiding the spy and Mei down the hall, keeping his hat low on his face.

The three guards were upon them in an instant. "What's happened?"

Jarron relayed the story, continuing toward the stairwell, finishing with, "You go check on the prisoner, I need to get them out of here."

The guards glanced at his uniform on the way by but were already racing toward the cell without pausing to look at his face.

The three escapees hurried up the stairs. Pushing through the barred door, Mei dropped the balled-up linens into a wet pile on the floor. A horrendous wall of odor wafted up from the linens.

False tears welled in her eyes. "It's really bad," she whispered.

The guards paled, coughing and gagging.

"Oh!"

"Urgh."

"Gods of hells."

Jarron pointed down the stairs. "The prisoner went mad and attacked us. They need backup."

Three of the six guards darted down the stairs.

Jarron started following the spy back toward the laundry.

"Where are you going?" the yellow-toothed guard demanded.

The spy's blood froze. To come this far and fail would be embarrassing. He prayed to X'era that Jarron could come up with something to say. Anything. In a maid's uniform, the spy couldn't reasonably answer for Jarron.

"To report the incident." Jarron glared.

The guard glared back for what felt like an eternity but finally waved them on.

Footsteps filled the hall as ten guards strode by. The spy bowed and pressed his back against the wall, hiding his face and clearing way. Mei copied him while Jarron gave a crisp salute.

"This way," the spy said after they passed.

They hurried toward the laundries as the palace filled with a flurry of activity. Shouts and alarm cries sounded far away. Somehow, they made it back to the laundry.

The spy stripped his uniform off and balled it into the pile of linens just outside the laundry. Mei shimmied out of her uniform and added it to the ball. They were left with their gardener's clothes.

"I better keep the uniform," Jarron said. "I have no spare clothes."

The spy nodded.

Glancing at the busy laundry, they skulked out the back door, creeping behind the linen carts. The spy spotted the nearly empty stables. They could get back to the gardens that way. He noted that many stable hands wore a brown cloak. He flipped his cloak inside out, and now wore a reddish-brown cloak.

Horse hooves clicked against the stones.

Jarron slipped back inside the laundry and the spy pressed Mei against the wall, concealing her behind his wall-colored cloak. The shadow did not turn inky or crackle, but magic was not the only way to be invisible.

Mei's eyes widened as she tucked her face into the crook of his shoulder. The spy edged closer, pressing his body against hers to keep her hidden. She looked up at him. His breath caught—realizing her body was pressed against the wall beneath his. And the way her eyes filled with heat; she'd just noticed it too. He swallowed and slowly backed away as the guards passed, creating space.

Nodding toward Jarron, who peered out from the doorway, the spy entered the stables.

The emperor walked past the spy.

Inhaling sharply, the spy motioned for Jarron to wait. Jarron's eyes widened before he darted outside the door. Mei lowered her head and grabbed a discarded watering can before slipping out another door.

The emperor paced outside the largest stall about to mount a midnight black horse wearing gilded bridle. The stallion stamped his feet and reared.

Trying to back away now might draw attention he couldn't afford. The spy reached down for a handful of hay, which he brushed over his cloak and hair. He selected a pitchfork leaning against the side of the barn to complete his disguise. Then he stepped into the main aisle. The spy's heart hammered as he came face-to-face with the emperor.

"Are you going to hold this godscursed beast still?" the emperor demanded of the spy.

He bowed low, keeping his face parallel with the floor. It would be harder to remember his features from that angle.

Quietly, he said, "Your Imperial Majesty."

"How dare you speak to me? I should have your tongue cut from your mouth, you insolent peasant. Were you not informed of the rules?" the emperor snarled.

The spy bowed low, saying nothing, but held the bridle still as the emperor mounted the snorting, stamping animal.

Shouting profanities against all the gods, the emperor kicked the horse on. "Who is responsible for this! Where in all the hells is my army going?"

With the emperor now gone and galloping down the golden road, the spy discarded the pitchfork, brushed the hay from himself, and flipped the cloak back to green. Mei slipped out from behind the stables as they hurried toward the gardens. Jarron caught up moments later.

The spy found the hole in the hedge, and the three pushed through again. The thorns snagged their skin and clothes as their need to flee meant they were less careful on the escape.

They disappeared into the crowd and were gone.

REBELLION
CHAPTER TEN

Walking out of the bakery, the nameless one wiped his charcoal-dusted hands on his flour-ridden apron. Today, he'd worked the ovens, which meant keeping the fires burning at the precise temperature all day. Outside, Mei was waiting for him, a bright grin on her face. She waved him over.

The spy strolled down the wall she perched on. "You're not very discreet," he observed.

She slipped off the wall, nearly close enough they were touching, eyeing him. She slid her hands onto his hips, pulling him closer.

Mei pressed her lips to his ear. "They'll just assume we're having a wild fling."

His brows shot up.

He leaned in and whispered in her ear, "So tonight, when you're dragging me to whatever rebel meeting you're headed to, they'll think we're tangled up in someone's sheets."

A peal of laughter escaped her lips. "How did you know!" She released his hips and batted his shoulder.

He chuckled. "You have a promise to make good on. I gave you Jarron, and now you give me the shrine."

"As promised." She glanced at him. "Do you need to change or?"

Before the spy answered, he noticed Jun watching him. The expression was hungry, too hungry for a casually interested recruit. Jun had asked him about the rebellion again during their shift and now watched the spy and Mei with an expression that caused the back of the spy's neck to prickle. Jun was his friend, or was he?

Glancing around he noticed a handful of others watching them with far too much interest for his liking. Some of them guards.

"It's fine. Go with this," the spy said.

"Wha—"

He cut her off with a quick kiss. As he pulled away, and she blinked slowly frozen in place.

"We have eyes on us," he murmured.

She swallowed. "We'll lose them in the market."

He slung his arm over her shoulders. They were nearly the same height, but he puffed himself up to manage it. It's what the Feng persona would have done.

Strolling through the hanging carpets and curtains of the market-place, Mei took them on a wild path between the cramped booths. Darting into a small courtyard with a well, Mei opened a weathered door and ushered him inside.

They entered a small apartment, and Mei closed the door behind them. Glancing out the window through curtains embroidered with flowers and dragons, Mei surveyed the courtyard.

The spy, instead, studied her apartment. Though modest, color burst from every corner. A clay vase of bright wildflowers soaked in the sun from the window in the kitchenette beside a small box of fresh herbs and jars of jam. The straw bed was neatly made with red, purple, and fire orange bedding. Woven rugs covered every inch of the floor. A shelf held small glass, stone, and jade trinkets beside dried lotus flowers.

"One of them is still out there, but I have another way out," Mei said.

Mei climbed out a window into a curved alley between the stone and wood apartments. The spy stepped out, leaning against the wall and peering out into the marketplace.

"Have we lost them?" she whispered.

"They're circling, but there's no one out here," he said.

She led the spy into a hidden door in the adjoining building, and through a forgotten hallway between the ground level apartments. They exited onto the street, donning colorful head wraps of dazzling patterns from one of the vendor booths. She led him into another building and another. They shed the first disguises, wearing variations as they slipped through the city.

She was learning quickly, keeping up with the disguises.

Finally, they entered a cramped upstairs room above a loud tavern. The peephole windows of the room were hidden underneath roof tiles and stonework. The spy hadn't noticed the third level from the street. It was perfectly hidden in plain sight.

The room was packed with people wearing face masks and various assortments of clothing. A large tapestry map hung from the ceiling against the wall. The spy approached it as Mei whispered harshly with one of the rebels.

The spy studied the old map. The seventeen nations, and three more that weren't on any maps he'd seen recently.

The man Mei had been whispering with approached. "We've gathered as many of the old maps of Teridar as we could and hidden them. The emperor will have a hard time finding whatever it is that he is searching for. Hopefully, that will accomplish whatever you're after, and we can use it as well."

"What happened to the three nations that have been erased from the new maps?" the spy asked.

"The nations that stood against him were erased from more than just the maps. No trace remains." The man grunted. "The homes and cities were burned to rubble five years ago. Vines have already started to overtake them as if they were never here. I hear you've been a thorn in the emperor's side. The army made it to the Infernal Falls, and the emperor was livid. You also freed Jarron—which I didn't think was possible."

"Mei helped with all of that," the spy said.

The man's eyes bored into him. "She says that you're hardly more than a shadow. Moving from place to place without being seen. Disappearing. Is that true?"

More than you realize.

The spy turned from the map. "You promised me information."

The man crossed his arms. "What are you going to do with the information?"

The spy bristled. "I gave you what you want. I expect the same in return."

The man stroked his chin thoughtfully.

A handful of warrior personas pushed through, and the spy found himself raising to his full height and width. "I will tell you that I do not wish for the emperor to continue to rule or invade other nations. I want to overthrow him and his false goddess."

The man held out his hand. "I'm Guo. What's your name?"

Mei slid between them. "The best spies don't use their names. The best spies don't even have names."

She glanced at the spy for confirmation. He nodded seriously, enjoying how gravely she took it.

"Well then what do we call you?" Guo's tone was flat.

"I am currently using the alias Feng."

Guo scratched his chin. "There is a place that fits what you described to Mei. The pyramid beside Niamh's temple has a maze within a maze, but it's rumored to have a large open space in the heart. It's been called the shrine."

Finally—an answer. He'd figure out a way to destroy or stop the creation of the Mooncursed. At the very least, he could try and delay it or find a way to stop them. Then he'd return to Avyllon.

His thoughts turned to the pyramids.

"The pyramid has no entrances," the spy said, having discarded it as a possibility after failing to find any doorways.

"The entrance is underground," Guo said. "Jiang's great grandfather was one of the builders on the project."

A man lifted his hand—Jiang.

Before the spy could ask, Guo said, "We assumed you would want help entering the pyramid?"

The spy nodded slowly, knowing what came next. "And what do you ask for in return?"

"We want to interrupt the rations trains for the army. If they can't eat, they can't invade maintain their power over the conquered nations." Guo winked. "Or invade anyone else."

"Fine. You find information on Niamh, and Mei and I will try to sabotage the Mooncursed," the spy said. "And I'll help you with the rations."

"Mei?" Guo tilted his head. "There are a number of rebels who could accompany you. Spies with more training."

"I work with Mei."

"Mei? You really should—"

"I *only* work with Mei," he stated firmly. "She's proven resourceful, a quick study, and has instincts that can't be taught."

Mei glanced up.

Guo lifted his hands. "Fine. But Jiang will accompany you tomorrow night. Meet at the pyramid."

The spy bowed. "Thank you."

"Is there anything else you can tell us, Feng?"

The nameless one paused, thinking back to the Mooncursed beasts with their gnashing fangs, tormented bodies, and pained eyes. He should warn them.

"The emperor has brought back the Mooncursed," he said. "I've seen them. If the guards are willing to behead people in the streets, you don't want to see what the Mooncursed can do. People should be warned."

Guo furrowed his brows. "We've heard the stories but haven't seen them."

Snapping, broken fangs. Metallic claws. Hulking beats with glowing yellow eyes. The screams and smears of blood.

"We'll never overthrow him while he's creating them," the nameless one said.

"I want to know why we aren't focused on killing him." A woman slammed her fist against a table.

The spy looked up. "I suspect there is some magic protecting him."

Serious expressions twisted on the masked faces.

The spy looked out the slit of a window toward the darkening city. Giving the information away was uncomfortable, but necessary. Hopefully, Aurienne would reply soon, and he'd have more direction.

"Thanks for the information. I'll be in touch," the spy said.

He and Mei left the cramped room and walked together. Her shoulders nearly brushed his beneath the fading dust. He peered at her from the corner of his eye, catching her glance his way more than once.

How many nights had he walked alone? Hundreds? More? Relishing the company, he realized just how lonely he had been. Maybe a permanent partner would be nice. After returning to Avyllon, he could reach out to Mei and see if she wanted to join him on missions.

When they reached the halfway mark between their apartments, Mei stopped.

She picked her fingernail. "You really want to work with me?"

He remembered the first time his Pa invited him on a mission that he'd actually been able to help on. The feeling of pride at being useful, being wanted. He knew exactly what she was feeling.

"Yes," he said genuinely. "You'll be an incredible spy or thief one day if you choose. More than that, I trust you. You've had my back."

"I won't let you down, I promise."

"I'll see you tomorrow," he waved.

"Remember, if anyone at work asks, I was amazing tonight!" she called out far too loudly.

He chuckled.

Chaos.

She strolled toward her apartment, lithe limbs swaying easily and hair flipping in the breeze. His heart twinged a little as he watched her go.

Returning to his apartment, he washed, changed, and ate a loaf of bread with some chicken stock and apples.

He placed an apple onto the windowsill, and whispered, "X'era, thank you for saving me when I was lost, for coming for me in the place between worlds. Thank you for your gifted ring, tethering me to this world. I will unmask this false goddess in your name. I am your humble servant."

His bed beckoned, but instead he located an inky shadow and found the quiet place in his mind.

He stepped through the shadows.

It felt different this time. The shadow clung to his body, making time feel slow. His hands and feet started to hurt, so he pushed back through the shadow to return. It fought him. He clawed through the shadows, finally falling to the floor.

He glanced up. The sun had long set and the stars twinkled in the sky. He'd lost hours in what felt like seconds. Both his hands faded in and out of view. Stumbling to his bed, he curled up into a ball and waited for his hands to return.

He'd only been inside moments. Why did the shadows linger? Why was he losing himself? He hadn't even used shadows much that day. His heart fell. The more he used them, the more they fought to claim him—just like X'era had warned. Hopefully, he'd recover enough to use them tomorrow at the shrine.

The nameless one fell asleep before his hands returned.

THE SHRINE
CHAPTER ELEVEN

Jiang waited with Mei on the street beside the pyramid, leaning against the wall smoking. Both wore layered, long grayish clothing that blended into the rocky foundation walls of the nearby buildings. They looked around for him but hadn't glanced upward yet. Few people thought to.

He waited. He didn't see anyone following them or lurking nearby. There were no waiting guards or rebel scouts posted anywhere. While he didn't believe Mei would betray him, he didn't know Jiang or Guo —and this could very well be a trap. He believed their interests aligned, but he'd been wrong before and couldn't afford that mistake now. A few more minutes just to be sure.

The nameless one studied the monument from a nearby rooftop, scouting every detail. Several hundred human-height steps cut into the crimson and gold step-pyramid, creating a zigzagging pattern into the sky. Trenches with oil lit the edges of the pyramid at each level.

Near the top was a single large egress, though he'd never seen anyone up there. He studied the painted designs on the pyramid walls, now noticing small slits in the stone that could let in light. It was made to look impenetrable, and it did. But now that he knew of the secret entrance, the cracks in the façade were beginning to show.

He'd been watching the pyramid for over an hour before Jiang and Mei showed up. In that time, he hadn't noticed anyone coming or going. The underground entrance had to be nearby. He fingered the hem of his cloak. He had no idea what he ought to be wearing. They'd have to fashion disguises quickly on the spot.

The worst plans are those without enough planning.

And all his recent missions of late hadn't had near enough planning. One day his skills and luck wouldn't be enough.

The nameless one shifted on the red tile rooftop to ease his cramping legs, glancing around as a prickling sensation skimmed his neck. He had a bad feeling about this, but this was his chance to get inside. If they had to come back later more prepared, then they had to come back later. At least he'd learn where the entrance was. He'd do as much reconnaissance as he could tonight and then get out. All plans started somewhere.

Then why does it feel like this is a horrible mistake?

He twisted X'era's ring absently. It slithered around his finger like it was a part of his skin. Invisible. If he focused, he could almost feel a magical tether anchoring him. Before joining the others, he needed to see whether he could enter the shadow world from outside the temple.

He leapt from the rooftop to an adjoining roof. Kicking his legs over the edge, he climbed down the building to the alley below. Finding the quiet calm in his mind, he found an inky shadow behind a box. He stepped into the shadow, into the dusky shadow world, and slipped toward the pyramid. There were no inky shadows there, just like at the palace and temples. Something barred his magic. He circled the building until his arms burned as his body struggled against the unnatural realm. It was weaker here than the temple and palace, but still present.

Godsdamn it all to the hells.

Returning to Jiang and Mei, he stepped out of a shadow beside a knobby cherry tree.

"Are you ready?" the spy asked.

Jiang whirled, drawing a dagger. "Where did you come from?"

The spy shrugged, noticing the twinkle in Mei's eyes.

She pulled her cloak over her head. "One day you'll show me how you do that."

"This way," Jiang said.

Jiang led them away from the illuminated pyramid toward the stone buildings surrounding it. The buildings were granaries, water storage, blacksmiths, tanners, and weavers. All professions. The spy studied them, now seeing they subtly differed from the neighboring structures. They were the same type of marbled stone as the pyramid. He hadn't noticed the difference before because the city had been built and rebuilt over time and was constructed with dozens of materials and architecture styles.

The nameless one stopped, sensing an oily presence looming around the pyramid, one that made the ring on his finger burn.

He whispered, "I sense there is something dangerous here. Magical."

"What?" Mei whispered. "I don't feel anything."

"Niamh," the nameless one replied coolly. "She's a devil in disguise. A false goddess. I won't rest until every effigy, every temple, is destroyed." The bite of his tone surprised him.

He'd never been very devout before, but he was finding that his new goddess inhabited a generous place in his mind. Her catlike eyes and divinely tall form with her billowing silver hair and shadow clothing were all burned into his memory.

Mei chewed her lip before tugging the face mask hanging at her neck over her mouth.

Jiang stopped at a small stone building with a wooden door facing the pyramid. It could have been an outhouse or storage shed. It connected to the back of an old mill, hiding under a thatched awning.

Hiding in plain sight.

The spy glanced around. There were old tracks in the dried mud. This doorway received frequent use. They'd have to be careful.

Their guide gestured to the door. "I don't have the key."

The spy began to draw his lock picking tools from a secret pocket in his pants.

"Can I try?" Mei asked hopefully.

He handed her the slim steel tools, and she got to work.

"That one slides in and holds the teeth up, and that one works under the next tooth. There you go," he said.

"I have—done this—before," she retorted.

He crossed his arms, concealing a grin. "You had me fooled."

She narrowed her eyes at him. "Pretend I'm making the gesture at you."

"What gesture?" Jiang whispered.

"Never mind," the spy said.

The lock clicked open.

"Got it!"

"Impressive," he said.

"How fast can you do it?"

The spy allowed himself to grin. "I can do it with my hands tied behind my back and blindfolded in a third the time."

She gaped.

Jiang rolled his eyes. "Can we do this?"

"After you," the spy said.

It was never a good idea to let someone you didn't trust behind you.

Jiang grunted and pushed open the door. It opened to a descending staircase leading into the yawning dark. Mei used the flint to light their torches. While she worked, striking flint on steel, the spy noted that he could see nearly perfectly in the dark now. He hardly needed the torches anymore, but he didn't want Jiang learning that.

"Here." Mei handed him the last torch.

They descended the stone stairs deep into the belly of the earth. The halls were wide enough for four people to walk side by side and the ceilings were high enough that the spy couldn't reach up and touch them. The spy pushed forward to lead the way.

Steady breaths.

The spy whispered to Mei. "Try to keep a map in your head of where we've been. Remembering the turns also helps, but it's not as efficient."

The trio crept through the halls, hiding in the many odd rooms when they heard voices. Inside the pyramid there were no doors, just an unending mountain of stone.

The spy froze, holding up his hand and listening.

Clicking and quiet snarling. The spy waved Mei and Jiang back into a nearby room to hide. They obeyed, pressing themselves against the wall near the door and dousing the torches. The spy cracked the seal on a vial he'd bought from a witch that masked scent against wolves and bears, hoping it worked on these beasts. He splashed it on his neck and offered it to his companions.

A Mooncursed beast that had to crouch to not graze its head along the ceiling crept through the tunnels. Patches of fur revealed metal bones and bone ridges. It wore a spiked titan ore collar. Its front leg dragged as it patrolled. The bony tail had no fur, just stacked bone spikes—like a rat's tail. Lifting its head, it sniffed, but continued.

They were in the right place.

The Mooncursed passed, and they waited long minutes.

"Those things..." Jiang stammered.

Mei paled.

"This way," the spy motioned them forward.

They hadn't learned anything about this place, except that it was a maze, and there were Mooncursed here. He needed more. They continued through the maze for two hours, stopping, hiding, retracing. The spy had formed a map in his head by this point. Torches lined the walls every fifteen paces, and he darted from shadow patch to shadow patch—though none turned inky.

He whispered to Mei. "There are three overlapping mazes. The outer maze and the inner maze are both connected by a series of dead ends. They weave together, so either think about it as two connected mazes or three with the weaving being its own. It's the most unpredictable and asymmetrical."

"What's the point of all this?" Jiang asked.

"There's something big at the center. And I think it's this way," the spy pointed.

A large doorway, twice as tall as the others, emerged from the end of the hall. The spy peered around the corner.

The ceiling was nearly as tall as the pyramid itself, and he could see the stacked shape of the structure. Balconies overlooked the room from above—crawling with wardens. Pillars carved to resemble firewyrms held up the ceiling.

And then he saw the cages.

The victims.

The experiments.

Thousands of titan ore cages held snarling Mooncursed. A large stone altar, the size of a house, had a dazed priestess of Niamh at all four sides. They stood over screaming victims caught in the throes of transformation.

They were making Mooncursed from *people* combined with *animals*.

A sick, churning feeling entered his gut as the blood ran from his face. They were kidnapping citizens or taking advantage of those claiming to be faithful or taking those they arrested even and bringing them here to turn them into monsters.

Severed limbs dripping black blood hung on butcher hooks. Overlapping screams and cries crowded the dank air. Bones cracked. Hammers pounded. Giant screws were turned as metal was fastened onto bone. Titan ore collars were locked onto unconscious beasts who were dragged into the cages by the armored, once-human wardens. The room reeked of old blood and corpses.

A warden removed his helmet, and the spy's breath caught. The wardens were corrupted too. More human than beast, they had metal plates, small bone ridges, and slightly distended limbs. Only partially changed, they were the more human versions of the ghastly Mooncursed. The emperor's advisor, Eryx, circled the altar, pouring an unknown black bubbling substance into the wounds of the victims.

The spy backed away as Mei and Jiang peered around the corner. Jiang spun and immediately vomited. Mei was shaking and leaning against the wall, tears streaming down her face. The spy retreated to one of the rooms they'd been hiding in, and his companions followed.

"I have never seen something so evil in my entire life. What is that?" Jiang hissed.

"That's what I came here to find out. I need to know how they're making them so I can stop them," the spy said.

"I can't... those are people... I know them. We have to help them." Mei's voice trembled.

"We've taken enough risk tonight," the spy said. "We need to get out and then regroup. Come up with a plan to find out exactly how they're making them. It has to do with those priestesses. We can follow one, maybe question one, and learn more information. If we get caught though, they're going to kill us. We have to leave."

Claws clicked on the stone floors. The spy, Mei, and Jiang froze. The spy's heart thumped inside his chest, as his blood ran cold.

Mooncursed.

Mei's hands shook as she pressed them against her mouth. Tears dripped down her face as she locked eyes with the spy. Her wide-eyed gaze held fearful, silent questions even as the line of her brow told him she'd follow his lead no matter what it was. He held his finger to his mouth. She nodded, though tears trickled down her cheeks.

Click.

Click.

Scrape.

Click.

It was coming closer. Quite rumbling snarls echoed through the maze. None of them dared move in case they were heard. Jiang glanced at the spy and then at the Mooncursed. He raised his dagger. The spy shook his head.

They'd never survive a fight with the Mooncursed. Their only option was to hide, or to run.

Click.

Scrape.

Clunk.

Not even daring to breathe, the spy silently mapped their location in his head. The Mooncursed was coming from the outer maze, patrolling the perimeter. Once it passed, they could double back from where it had come and retrace their steps to the entrance. If it didn't... their only route was farther into the inner maze—directly back toward the cursed heart where thousands of Mooncursed waited in those cages.

The Mooncursed paused near the opening between the mazes. The spy willed the shadows to cover them. He wasn't sure if it was possible, but he had to try.

Please, X'era.

The Mooncursed continued past the access and toward the maze. Relief flooded the spy. Jiang swallowed and exhaled a shuddering breath.

The Mooncursed stopped, sniffing the air. It turned toward their hallway—glowing yellow eyes snapping to the pool of vomit. Its eyes narrowed to scorching slits, and it bared its fangs in a snarl.

"Run," the spy whispered.

The spy grabbed Mei's hand and took off toward the inner maze. Jiang was a second behind them, scrambling through the turns. The spy was like smoke over water, gliding from turn to turn, following the map in his head. Jiang was starting to fall behind. The spy took another turn, and Jiang wasn't there.

The spy slowed, hissing, "Jiang!"

Jiang turned the corner, panting. A massive metal-clawed paw reached around the corner and struck his head from his shoulders.

Mei froze and started to scream, but the spy dragged her farther into the maze. Even a moment's hesitation would cost them their lives. He raced through the pyramid as warning bells sounded. The deafening gonging noise echoed through the stone, and the spy's ears threatened to burst.

Snarls and scraping filled the halls on all sides. They would soon be trapped. The spy looked down one hall and then the other. Both had Mooncursed. There was no way out. Frantically, he searched for an inky shadow, but none appeared.

Mei's hand quivered in his, and her wide eyes never left his face.

Godsdamn it.

He couldn't let her die like this. He pushed her into an alcove. It was a tight fit—not made for humans, but Mei was slim enough to fit if she wedged herself inside.

"I'm going to draw them away," he said. "As soon as they pass, you run that way. Left, right, right, left, right, right, left, left, left and you'll hit the stairwell. Don't let them see you. Do you understand?"

Her voice cracked. "How're you going to get away?"

"I'll find a way. I'm a master spy, remember? I appear and disappear, and I'm going to be fine. Now tell me what I just said."

"Left, right, right, left, right, right, left, left, left to the stairwell," she stammered.

"Good. And once you get out you run home. You don't wait for me. You don't come looking for me. I'll find you." He pressed a quick kiss to her forehead.

Her eyes widened. "I can't just leave you here."

"You have to. Pretend you're invisible. Find the quiet place inside your mind, in your soul. Calm your breathing and your heart. Let your limbs go slack. Pray to X'era." The spy blew out the nearby torch on the wall, shrouding her in darkness.

Be safe.

Running, he dragged his unlit torch along the walls. It clanged and dinged over the mortar and stones—echoing through the structure. He had to force his footsteps to be loud, else years of practice would have made them quiet.

Ding.

Clang.

Clank.

Ding.

But then the empty halls filled with sounds that struck icy fear into his heart.

Click.

Scrape.

Clunk.

Thud.

Click.

They'd surrounded him. He continued running, but he knew they were coming from all sides. He darted toward the outside pyramid loop, doubling back and slipping between the mazes. Darting into a dark room, he waited for several Mooncursed to race by before he doubled back again.

Lead them away from Mei. As far as I can get.

He led them toward the center of the pyramid, and they were gaining fast. He skidded away from the main entrance into the massive room with the columns and the cages.

"Release them! Find him," someone shouted.

Metal clanged as the cage doors sprang open.

Hundreds of Mooncursed raced for him, and he hadn't come through these halls on the way in. He was lost, surrounded, trapped as he hit a dead end.

Mindlessly, he beat his hands against the stone walls to no avail. He spun, hearing snarls just outside the dead end.

There was nowhere to hide. Nowhere to run. Except... he glanced at one of the shadows in the room. The one sitting on a puddle of dark water so still that not even a ripple broke the reflective surface. Something prevented any of the shadows from taking on that oily sheen he'd grown accustomed to, but the first shadow he'd fallen into looked just like that one. Why wasn't it a shadow door?

He ran to it, stopping at the surface. It didn't look like it went on forever, like the portals.

What is different?

A Mooncursed turned the corner, entering the room. Saliva dripped from its jagged fangs, hissing as it hit the ground. Metal claws dug deep gouges into the stone. It snarled and prepared to pounce.

The ring on his hand warmed.

The ring!

X'era's gift kept him tethered to this world. Even if something was blocking magic in the pyramid, if he took it off... The Mooncursed launched at him, claws extended. He didn't have time to finish the thought. He palmed the ring and stepped into the watery shadow.

Claws raked his cloak, and he fell.

RATIONS
CHAPTER TWELVE

Falling between worlds the second time was nothing like the first. The nameless one clasped X'era's ring in his fist and pressed it to his chest. Last time, not so long ago and yet a lifetime away, he'd fallen through oceans into clouds between floating islands before landing among all those sealed doorways.

This time he floated between cities trapped in giant bubbles. Whales the size of mountains sang their songs. He brushed up against a veil, sliding through it, he was in a forest. The trees touched the stars, and droplets of water were portals to smaller worlds. Brushing up against another veil, he entered another realm.

Wonder and awe overtook his ability to think.

Flying beings of light fluttered between rainbow planets. Ancient stone doorways opened to dazzling cities with flying carriages and glass buildings. In another world, winged, horned horses galloped through lavender fields. Another world was so old, it had died and all that remained was a crimson necropolis with shattering earthquakes. He passed into yet another world where fluffy floating wisps sparked with seafoam-colored lightning.

Sound became color, and time lost all meaning. He could float through these worlds forever. His chest burned, but he pushed the pain aside as he drifted through the realms.

Softly, someone called his name. The shock of hearing his true name for the third time in his life dragged him from his dreamy reverie. Blinking, he tried to think. His thoughts came crashing back. He knew that voice.

"X'era? X'era, are you there?" he called.

"Come back, my child. You've gone too far," the voice replied distantly.

"X'era, where am I?" He looked around, starting to panic. "How do I get back to the place between worlds?"

Her voice was so far away. "Come back, child."

The ring in his palm sizzled his skin, leaving a circular mark. Emersed in his fall, he'd forgotten about it, but her words reminded him of the precious gift. Carefully, he slid the ring on his finger.

The world came crashing back.

He was in the shadow world again, the mirror to his world. He was just outside the pyramid. Shaking, he stepped through one of the slits of light that marked the passages back.

It was early afternoon. But that couldn't be right, it had been nighttime when they'd entered the palace. How much time passed this time?

Mei! Was she alright?

He stumbled through the streets, pushing through the crowd toward her house. He froze and turned slowly toward a calendar hanging from a lotus shop.

No. That can't be right. It's been over a week?

Fear speared him. It's been a week. A week he'd left Mei. Had she even gotten out? Had she been rotting in a dungeon this whole time?

He ran all the way to her apartment. He knocked on the door frantically, but no one answered.

"Do you know where Mei is?" he asked an old woman.

She lifted her brow. "Lover's spat?"

"Um, yes, and I need to apologize."

"You should bring her flowers. She's at the bakery today."

Relief filled every tired, half corporeal limb. She'd made it out of the pyramid. She was alive and at the bakery.

The bakery? Why was she there? She doesn't work at the bakery.

Realization hit him like an angry goat. She was covering for him, waiting for him. Immediately, he ran to the bakery, not caring if he attracted attention on the way. Blinking in and out of existence, he paced for over an hour before he regained his corporeal form.

He raced inside the enormous building, stopping at the assignment board. His brain didn't work. He couldn't remember what station he'd been assigned to.

The mixing station. He darted inside, grabbing an old apron off a hook. He ran down the aisle, dodging auditors as he hunted for Mei. He found her mixing the ingredients of dough at the end of one of the tables. He slid into the station across from her.

Her eyes lit up. "You're back! You're alright." Her expression darkened. "Where have you been?"

"Yes—I," he began.

"Do you know how long you've been gone? Where were you? I've been worried sick."

"I just made it back. I went looking for you the instant I got away," he whispered, now mixing dough for a loaf of his own.

"What do you mean you *just made it back*? You've been in the pyramid this whole time? Hiding?"

"Something like that." How could he explain where he'd been? "I just got away. I promise."

"I thought you would have cared what happened to me." She looked down. "And you've been gone. I thought you... left."

She had a reason to worry. How many times lately had he wanted to return to Avyllon and leave all of this behind? His heart ached that she thought he'd leave without saying goodbye at least. They were partners.

"I wouldn't leave like that," he said.

Her expression softened for a moment before it caught on something over the spy's shoulder. She nodded behind him.

"Someone is listening," she said.

"Bring your dough to the rising room," an auditor said to Mei.

She grimaced but followed them away.

The spy turned to find Jun glancing over his shoulder.

"You're back," Jun said.

"Yeah, I..."

"Was busy," Jun finished.

The spy's skin prickled. Jun was far too interested. Maybe the spy being gone for days at a time without warning coupled with his rebellious alias was that interesting. Or Jun's motives weren't entirely altruistic.

Jun worked his dough. "You should know that you missed a few days of work before Mei started showing up for you. And she was all beat up when she did. She's been waiting for you for days, acting strangely. Nervous. You shouldn't trust her."

Creating rifts between allies. It was a classic strategy, and one the spy should have expected. Driving wedges hurt alliances, rebellions, coupes.

He trusted Mei, but Jun's words had their intended effect and planted a tiny seed of doubt.

"Thanks," he said, not meaning it.

That meant Jun might be working with the emperor.

Mei returned with a new set of ingredients and got to work. She tugged her sleeve over a bandage, hissing.

She'd been injured.

He cursed.

Mei interrupted his train of thought and whispered, "The army returned."

Godsdamn it.

He had lost a week to the other worlds and was more behind than ever now. Avyllon needed more time.

"Guo has been waiting for you to make good on your offer to help disturb the supply lines," Mei whispered. "We go tonight."

Late that afternoon, the spy managed to locate the military supply shipment schedule from the army administrative offices. With a few strokes of ink, he reassigned the guards transporting the supplies and replaced them with his own fabricated ones—all rebels courtesy of Mei and Guo.

After a stunningly assertive performance by Mei where she dressed down the supply commander of the entire military, the rebels left the city with the supply caravan.

The ink and the person. Espionage always came back to those two things. The supply caravan was supposed to meet the returning army.

It wouldn't get that far.

The ornate pommel of the stolen saddle glistened as the spy rode down the golden road. Dozens of wagons followed.

The small turnoff was just ahead. They'd unload the supplies there and return with empty wagons. It would be an administrative nightmare that the auditors would never uncover. The army wouldn't be able to march through the isthmus to Avyllon, buying Aurienne weeks if not months to prepare. They turned down the small road.

It was all going according to plan. Until the sound of approaching hooves stopped the supply caravan in its tracks.

"I'll do the talking. No one make any rash moves," the spy hissed.

About twenty soldiers reined their horses to a stop before the spy, stallions snorting and stamping their polished hooves.

"Whoah," the front soldier said. "Where are you going?"

"Stopping to rest the horses," the spy replied. "We traveled through the night."

"We didn't hear anything about a stop ordered," the soldier said.

The spy shrugged. "We got a late start. The paperwork wasn't in order."

"We were sent to escort you. Our rations are running low," the soldier said.

Shitting gods of Nyx'ela.

His mind raced to think of an excuse they'd buy. "One of our wagons has a cracked wheel. We will need to repair it. Could you send for supplies?"

The soldier's gaze narrowed. "Don't you have repair supplies?"

Did they?

"I didn't see any." The spy shrugged.

"Leave the broken wagon. Let's get the rest of these to the army," the soldier said, circling his horse.

The soldier glanced between the spy and Guo, who was drifting closer. The spy squinted at Guo and brought his hand up against the light, pretending to shield his eyes while he was glaring and warning Guo to stand down.

"Is there a problem?" The soldier's hand tightened on the hilt.

"None at all," the spy said as brightly as he could. "I hear you. The army needs its food. We'll get those rations to your people and come back for the damaged wagon. We'll leave two soldiers here to guard the wagon until we return."

The soldier hesitated, studying Guo carefully.

The spy nudged his own horse forward. He reached into his cloak, fingers closing on the cool vial of blinding dust. They'd have to figure out how to spin this later, but at least—

A soldier squinted at Guo. "Don't I know you?"

Guo drew his sword and charged.

"No!" The spy cried.

Metal clanged.

Guo crossed swords with the captain. A soldier charged for the spy. The spy reined his horse out of the way and hurled a vial at him. The soldier fell from his horse, screaming and holding his face.

Another charged Mei, but she was staring at the screaming soldier and didn't see her coming.

The spy kicked his horse into a gallop. The soldier raised her sword and started to bring it down on Mei. He wouldn't make it in time. Mei's attention snapped up, and she dove from her horse's back. The sword clanked against the metal pommel, and Mei's horse reared. It kicked the solider in the chest, knocking her off her horse. She stood, rising her sword again as Mei scrambled away. Knives flicked from his wrists and sank into the woman's spine. She toppled beside Mei, blood trickling from the corner of her mouth.

When the spy turned back to the skirmish, twenty soldiers were already dead, having been outnumbered three to one with angry rebels.

Guo wiped his blade on a cloth. "We'll hide the bodies in the woods. This close to the Nyx'ela mountains, the shades and beasts will take care of them."

The spy's gaze snapped to Guo as anger burned inside his chest. Guo's comments were callous on deaths of soldiers who may not have wanted to join this war, who were following orders and trying to stay alive. They could have been turned or silenced.

The spy stormed up to the rebel leader. "I was going to dust them. They wouldn't have known what we were doing and would have recovered in days."

Guo shrugged. "People die in war."

The spy's hand went to his hilt. "Not when they don't have to. It leaves a trail we don't want."

Guo held his hands up and puffed out his chest, taunting. "You wanna try this?"

Yes.

After what he'd seen at the temple, he was so tired of bloodshed. The worlds were too grand, too magical to be wasting life. Anger rippled through him, but he released his hilt and instead leveled a flat stare at Guo.

The spy bent down and ripped his daggers from the soldier's back, stowing them into his sleeves with purposeful snaps. "This was *my* mission. The next time you deviate from the mission and end lives without my permission will make you my enemy."

The rebel leader drew his sword. "Is that a threat?"

An inky shadow beside the wagon winked at the spy.

Time to teach the rebel a lesson he'd never forget.

The spy spun, dissolving into the shadows and reappearing behind Guo. Roughly, he gripped the collar of Guo's uniform and pressed the dagger against his neck.

"Yes," the spy hissed.

The rebels drew their katanas. The spy pressed his blade a little closer. His other hand was blinking in and out of existence, but he managed to keep the other hand corporeal enough to hold the dagger. Guo froze before he held up his hand and sheathed his sword.

"Just a misunderstanding, everyone." Guo cast a dark glance over his shoulder and said, "We all understand each other now."

If the spy killed Guo, they'd attack him and maybe Mei. He might shadowstep and kill them all, but for what. Death was what he wanted to avoid, and they were just fighting for their freedom.

"There's been enough death," the spy said.

The spy withdrew his blade and slipped back into the shadow. He stepped out from behind the wagon near Mei—who he realized hadn't drawn her own knives during the encounter. Both hands blinked in and out of existence this time, and he stuffed them into his pockets.

Guo's eyes fell upon him. "You're not a man. You're a shade. A wraith," Guo said. "It's why you use no name. Shades have no name."

Guo didn't sound afraid. Wary or apprehensive, but not afraid. Like he'd taken the spy's measure and would decide what to do with that information later. The other rebels backed away.

Mei rubbed her arm absently, the one that had the bandage on it.

He frowned. "Is your arm alright?"

She tugged her sleeve down. "Let's get these wagons to the village and unloaded before any other soldiers come looking for them."

Retaliation
Chapter Thirteen

Sweat and dust coated the spy's skin and hair. The bed creaked under his weight, and he glared at the bathing tub and the effort required to clean the days of travel. They'd unloaded the rations in the village with plans to slowly sneak it back into the city. The empty wagons returned to the administrative offices. They'd pulled off the heist, but the deaths of the soldiers weighed heavily on him. He was no stranger to death, but it was so unnecessary, and where was the line between that and the dark deeds in the heart of the pyramid. Judging by Mei's silence on the ride back, something weighed heavily on her too.

The nameless one scrubbed his hands over his face and dragged his fingers through his short hair. He hadn't slept in days, after not sleeping when he'd fallen through the worlds at the pyramid. It felt like he hadn't slept in a week and maybe he hadn't. He wasn't sure how shadowstepping world-traveling time worked.

He leaned back on top of the faded, threadbare blanket. If he just closed his eyes for a minute, he could get just a little sleep—

Screams cut through the morning bustle. And then more screams. The spy's eyes popped open.

Click.

Scrape.
Clunk.
Thud.
Click.

The spy's chest clamped down around his lungs. He darted to the window, pushing back the curtains.

Titan-ore-clad wardens dragged Mooncursed beasts on leashes through the city. The spy froze as his blood hardened to an icy sludge. Needles of pain pricked his heart as he blinked and rubbed his eyes. Prowling monsters dripping black ichor stalked every street. There were hundreds.

People huddled in terrified groups, too afraid to even scream or shout.

"Bring your tax to your door," a warden announced.

"We just paid taxes a week ago. They aren't due for another three weeks," a woman yelled as she stormed outside, before freezing in her doorway with her mouth hanging open.

The warden loosened the leash, and the Mooncursed bit into her neck.

The spy's hand slammed against his mouth, and he stumbled away from the window.

The Mooncursed tore into her neck, shaking and ripping, and blood spurted everywhere. And then it started to *eat*.

"No arguments," the warden snarled. "No questions. The army didn't get their rations, and the emperor has ordered us to restock them so they can head to the isthmus immediately."

Another warden yanked on the Mooncursed's leash. "Any empty offering bowls will be met with our emperor's Mooncursed. Spread the word." One of her teeth gleamed gold.

People ran through the streets giving the warning. Others hid indoors. The spy watched a few people on his street dump food, sweets, coins, and other offerings into bowl after bowl.

"We don't have enough," a woman carrying a newborn cried as she handed a soldier a bag of gold.

A neighbor handed over several small bags. "Here you go."

The woman cut her finger and bled into an offering bowl.

Apparently, Niamh accepted blood as an offering.

Bang, bang, bang.

The spy palmed a dagger and opened his door. Mei burst in.

"Do you hear what they're doing?" she demanded. "What are we going to do?"

"How fast can Guo get the supplies back?"

"A few days..." she said. "A week maybe. But people don't even have enough to pay these new demands. People are going to starve."

Screams caught the spy's attention.

A warden dragged a man down the street. Other wardens dragged shouting people in the same direction.

The spy slipped out his window and began following on the rooftops. Mei was behind him, surprisingly keeping up as he leapt from roof to roof.

In a large public square, the people were dragged onto the roof of an audit building. The warden knotted a noose around the neck of the first man.

"They're not going to," Mei whispered. "They can't."

Crack.

The first man fell. Then another and another. Eight swinging bodies.

"Their offering bowls were empty," the warden said.

Chaos broke out. The spy was jostled roughly by the fighting and bartering. A shoulder slammed into him, then an elbow. He fought to push through the crowd. Offering bowls overflowed with gold and gems beneath his feet, and he danced to avoid stepping on the heaping, bloodstained piles.

Mooncursed attacked people in broad daylight, dragging them away. People screamed and ran from the chained beasts. Empty wagons were filled as people sobbed and begged for mercy.

The same wagons they'd used to steal the rations.

It all made sense. They'd been responsible for all of this. It was a message he received loud and clear.

"Go to Guo. We need those rations here as quickly as possible.

Maybe the emperor will stop attacking his own people if the rations are returned. We can find another way to delay the invasion."

Mei whirled on him. "All you talk about is the war. And Avyllon and all the other nations. But what about us?" She threw up her hands.

The spy's temper flared. "Everything I've done is for both. If he invades and has Avyllon's seers at his command, he will be unstoppable. How do you kill an enemy who can see you coming? I've been doing everything I can to weaken him. That helps us both."

"I don't know who you are," she hissed. "Who you're working for. I don't know anything about you. I don't even know your name. And now people are starving, dying because of you."

"Me? I did everything I could to stall him. Guo killed the soldiers, and it was his idea to disrupt the army rations. The emperor is kidnapping and corrupting citizens into monsters. And I—"

"What have you even done but buy *other* nations more time?" she demanded. "I thought you could help *us*. I believed in you."

Something clicked in her mind, which was evident on her face. The small changes in her expression. Bitterness in her eyes. The angry flare of her nostril. Sadness on the corners her mouth.

What did she expect? He was a spy. He wasn't a rebel leader, or a strategist. Spies found information and shared it with people who made the decisions. Except, he'd been here alone with no way to get new orders. He should have left when he had the chance.

He forced his voice to be calm. "He's too powerful. That's why we need to take him down."

She looked away. "I'll go talk to Guo. I'll see you later."

Mei strode off, clenching her fists. The spy watched her until she disappeared in the crowds as the icy needles of unease crept down his spine.

Blown Cover
Chapter Fourteen

Silence had always been the nameless one's old friend, but today it only made his small apartment feel lonely. He'd received no correspondence from Aurienne in weeks, and he suspected his letters hadn't been posted either. He'd sent birds, too, but they never returned. Ever since Emperor Rexil declared war on the continent of Teridar, their communications had been cut off. He'd had to resort to the slower spy networks, but those took too much time.

From behind his curtains, he watched imperial guards accompanied by wardens going house to house demanding tribute and taxes. More than anything, he wished for guidance. He'd tried his best, but it had all backfired horribly.

Mei's face was so disappointed when the first of the army began retaking supplies. Conflicted. Lost. He wished she didn't always look to him for the answers. Ever since the summit, he didn't have any. He'd been floundering and trying to keep the army from invading, but it had been setback after setback with luck barely pulling them through. And now, he had no idea what to do.

It might be time to return to Avyllon. If so, he'd invite Mei to come. If they were truly partners—she had the right to know every-thing. He'd tell her about the High Seer. He'd tell her the truth about shadowstepping and X'era. All of it. He'd never trusted anyone before with his secrets, and that would be trusting her with everything. If there was anyone he wanted to know, and to know him, it was his partner. Working together there was nothing they couldn't do. Once Aurienne gave them a directive for the rebellion, they could return and help destroy Demorra from the inside.

He hadn't seen Mei in a few days. They'd agreed to lay low while the army was resupplying. He'd find her and tell her the truth. Scanning his apartment, he realized this might be the last time he would see it. Strangely, he wouldn't miss it. Another place he stayed a while and left without a word. From the first step inside, he knew this wasn't home.

Maybe one day, after the war, he'd be done spying. He'd find a home, somewhere near Ma's house. He could bake bread and raise chickens and cows. It might be nice to have a place he'd miss. People to miss.

He smiled as he packed up a satchel of belongings. His entire life fit into the single bag. The rest he could replace.

The hairs on his neck prickled and not a moment too soon. He dove for an inky shadow under the bed as the door splintered inward. Wardens and Mooncursed beasts filled the room. The Mooncursed's claws raked the floors and walls, sniffing and searching.

Waiting in the shadow world, he watched, as Emperor Rexil stepped inside his cramped apartment.

The emperor opened a drawer of odds and ends, picking up the needle and thread before setting it down. He pushed back the curtain and peered outside for long moments, looking up and down and around. In the finest robes, he strode to the bed and sat on it. Hands reaching across the threadbare blanket, the emperor traced the holes and frayed edges. The bed groaned under his weight.

"It's so ordinary," the emperor said.

That's the point.

"I suppose that's the point," the emperor said at the same time.

The spy's heart leapt into his throat.

The emperor looked around the room, eyes passing over where the spy hovered in the shadow world. "He was just here. I sense his energy. Search the room. Search the surrounding buildings. Find him."

The emperor exited the apartment and the spy drifted away. He slipped through the city, until he was far enough away that he was sure the emperor's guards wouldn't find him. His chest started to burn, and he stepped out of a shadow.

He blinked in and out of existence.

Godsdamn it.

Cursing, he waited for his body to return. It was taking longer and longer each time. He needed to stop shadowstepping altogether if he wanted to retain his form. How had they found him? He had been practicing shadowstepping a few weeks ago, which had garnered a lot of notice, so it was possible that they'd finally found him. That didn't feel right though.

Someone had given him up. Someone who had been too interested in the rebellion, and who'd warned him against trusting Mei. He'd gotten a bad feeling about this person ever since he shadowstepped.

Jun.

Usually, he'd never think twice at betrayal. He had no reason to. But here... he cared about the city of Rexila. Mei had made him care. He wanted to help the people here, and the fact that they refused to help themselves by allowing the in-fighting and conquering and warbands continue for so long infuriated him. Maybe his grandfather had been right in leaving. He had to find out.

Grimacing, he set off toward Jun's neighborhood. He asked around until someone gave him Jun's address.

Children played in the small, well-kept garden outside his house. One child fed small seeds to a round chicken.

He waited for Jun to come outside, and then stepped away from a building folding his arms. As Jun noticed him, his expression grew somber.

"Go inside, children," Jun said.

Three giggling children chased the orange and white chicken in the house.

Jun wiped his hands on a rag and approached. "Feng. This doesn't look like a social call."

"My house was tossed today. Someone told the emperor where I lived and gave him cause to look for me," the spy said.

He clenched and unclenched his fists as his fingers flickered in and out of this realm.

Jun crossed his arms. "I don't even know where you live. Why would you assume I had anything to do with it?"

"You asked about the rebels. You warned me against trusting them."

"I told you what I saw, nothing more," Jun said. "And I meant what I said about the rebellion. You see those children in there? I don't want them worrying about their next meal. I don't want them sleeping in my bed because they've heard monsters prowling the streets at night. I don't want my wife and our mothers to keep constant watch on all of them because people are disappearing. I don't want them executed in the street because they forgot to drop a few coins in that godsdamned offering bowl."

Tongues of Nyx'ela and all its gods, he sounded like he was telling the truth.

The spy pinched the bridge of his nose. He'd been under cover so long he didn't even know who to believe any more.

Jun stepped forward. "I've been supporting the rebellion where I can. You would know that if you were truly part of them. You'd know I wouldn't give up any of them. I have too much to lose."

The spy leaned against the building, shaking his head. Had he been wrong about all of his suspicions? Had Jun been his friend after all?

Gods of death.

He wanted to believe it so badly. For now, he'd have to accept it. He didn't know enough to do anything otherwise.

"Be careful, friend. There are whispers of something happening today," Jun said.

"Take care of yourself," the spy said.

If Jun didn't give him up... he couldn't even think about that right now. He had to find Mei and make sure she was safe. If they'd somehow found him, they might have found her too.

He started walking, then jogging. What if she was in the dungeons? He couldn't shadowstep in the palace. Or worse, what if she'd been taken to the pyramid?

"Everyone gather! Imperial announcement!" guards shouted through the streets.

He slowed to a walk to avoid a wall of imperial guards, and he tugged his hood over his head.

"Announcement! Proceed to the palace or your nearest announcer's stand," guards yelled.

Crowds pushed the spy in the direction of the palace. He was caught up in the throngs, and going against them would only draw attention. With a glance in the direction of Mei's apartment, the spy was swept away.

Betrayal
Chapter Fifteen

Quiet, packed crowds gathered in the tens of thousands before the imperial palace for miles in every direction. The spy leaned against a building in the alleyway.

The bells sounded, and the emperor appeared on the balcony. "Citizens of Rexila city, the nations of Teridar have refused to join the empire of Demorra. Peace talks have been unsuccessful. They declared war."

The spy's brow floated upward.

That was an interesting take on the conversation.

"The army prepares to leave," the emperor declared. "We have had rebels and spies in our midst, thwarting our attempts to answer the declaration of war. But rest assured, these have been dealt with."

The spy's blood chilled, and he glanced around.

"Have there been arrests?" he asked someone nearby.

The man shrugged.

The spy drifted through the crowd. "Have there been arrests?" he asked again.

"There were a few big raids last night," a woman with a child on her hip answered. "My friend's husband was taken."

The emperor continued, "We are stronger together. The empire will crush its enemies. Military drafts and new taxes have been posted. Failure to adhere to these will result in arrest. Failure to abide by the offering laws will result in death by fang."

The emperor returned inside.

Mei.

The spy raced toward her apartment. The crowd remained whispering and gathering, so it took him over an hour, even with shadow-stepping. He stopped outside the building, studying it from a nearby garden. There were people posted on adjacent rooftops in dark cloaks, watching the streets.

Spies.

His heart sank. The spies wouldn't be watching her, not with the widespread rebel arrests. They would have just arrested her. They were using her to get to someone else. He had a sickening feeling they were using her to get to him.

Mei, what have you done?

He thought about walking away. Leaving her. Leaving the city. Returning to Avyllon. He hesitated. The people of this city, of this continent needed him. If he left, he'd be abandoning them to this fate. He'd be failing X'era. Maybe Mei was in trouble and needed him. Could it be that she hadn't betrayed him? He'd at least give her a chance.

He swallowed, regretting that he'd ever trusted her.

Please let me be wrong.

The spy stepped into a glimmering shadow and half-floated through the shadow world until he found her. She was sitting outside in a small garden beside a water well. Her head was down, and she fiddled with her hem.

He stepped out of a shadow to sit beside her.

"I was worried they arrested you," he said.

She jumped. "Where did you come from?"

He might have smiled under any other circumstances. "Why are there spies watching your house?"

Her face fell, and she sagged onto the small wooden bench.

"Do you need help?"

Her lip quivered. It was all the confirmation he needed about what she'd done.

"Ah." He pursed his lips and frowned.

"I..."

"Why?" he asked.

"What?"

"Why did you give me up?" He picked a blade of grass rooted between two cobblestones.

She stood, pacing the small courtyard. "The night at the pyramid, I didn't get away. The Mooncursed caught me. Scratched me—infected me."

A weight crashed onto him. After all he'd done to try to save her that night, he'd failed, slipped into the shadow realm, and left her alone. Understanding cut through him.

"The scratch, they were going to make me one of those things. They said I'd turn if it wasn't cleansed before the full moon. I... I can't..." She bowed her head. "I wasn't going to say anything about you, but they said they'd release some of the prisoners. They freed some of them. They promised to free more if they captured you."

She tugged at a bandage on her arm.

"And they won't give you the cure until they have me?"

She nodded slowly, refusing to meet his eyes. "Worse. With this infection, they'll find me no matter where I go. They'll bring me back, sew on body parts of beasts, and let the transformation complete. I already feel the change beginning. Even if I could run from them, I fear it won't matter."

The spy looked at his hands, winking in and out of existence. For weeks, he'd been terrified of turning into a monster. It was hard to fault her for fearing the same thing after seeing the horrors in the pyramid.

She wasn't trained to withstand questioning. He'd left her alone there, and she'd done what she needed to survive. This is why he always worked alone. In the end, he couldn't count on anyone else.

"They told me you were a spy for Avyllon here to destroy us. You were trying to weaken our people... I didn't believe it at first but then with the rations..."

"You believed them."

The rations and the retaliation did look exactly like infrastructural sabotage. He couldn't have planned it better if he tried, no matter his intent. His mistakes piling up threatened to crush him now.

She sank onto the edge of the well. "I didn't know what to believe."

Her eyes searched his, looking for answers, for something he couldn't give her. All his answers would come too late.

"I work for the High Seer of Avyllon, but they're wrong about what I've been doing. I didn't send the army away and help with the rations because I wanted to weaken you. Maybe I should have guessed the emperor would retaliate, but I didn't. And my plans for the shrine were to keep from happening exactly what happened with the Mooncursed. I never wanted to hurt the people of Demorra. I want to overthrow the emperor to protect you all, and Avyllon too. I just couldn't do it alone. I thought with you..." He shook his head.

Tears slipped down her face as her features twisted in anguish.

It didn't matter now.

"When are they coming?" he asked.

"They'll be here any minute. You could still run."

"And you wouldn't get your cure. I'll go. Maybe they'll actually keep their word and release the prisoners."

"But you'll die."

It was true. He hadn't been able to shadowstep in the palace before, and he knew the dungeons were all but inescapable from the inside. If he went with them, he might not escape. Glancing at the rooftops, this might truly be his last chance at freedom. His last chance to leave this all behind.

It meant allowing Mei become a Mooncursed for betraying him. He couldn't do it. His shadows might not have worked in the palace before, but he'd freed a prisoner from those dungeons before. There was a small chance he'd be able to do it again, and he had to risk it.

For the first time, he had something to lose.

"And you'll die if I don't," he said.

They sat there for long minutes until the sounds of armor clanging met them. He stood.

His father and grandfather met this same fate. He only hoped he'd be as brave as they were.

"Keep your hands up!" Wardens filled the small space with swords drawn.

The spy ambled toward them, complying.

"You never told me your name," she whispered.

"I don't break under torture." He meant it as a joke, but it came across flat.

She flinched at the crack of his words.

The guards were nearly upon him when he said, "It'll be that much easier to forget me if you don't know. Besides, the best spies don't have names."

His words hit their mark.

She clutched her chest as sobs wracked her body. Even in the face of her betrayal, hurting her stung.

"Goodbye Mei."

His brain worked to form a plan. He'd wait long enough for her to get the draught and disappear. After giving her a few hours, he'd slip through the shadows. If he removed his ring, he might be able to shadowstep even inside the palace. There was a risk he'd fall between worlds again, but maybe he could escape. Or he would die.

Wardens stepped forward, gripping the spy. The titan ore gauntlets burned his skin, like hot bubbling oil. He searched for that quiet place in his mind where the shadow world would open, but the burning in his arms pushed it away.

Titan ore negates magic.

He'd never known why they used it on the Mooncursed, why the wardens wore titan ore armor, or why it covered the palace and temples, but now it all made sense. He couldn't shadowstep to escape. He was trapped.

For the first time—he was truly afraid.

X'era, help me.

Torment
Chapter Sixteen

Chained to a wooden chair by titan ore shackles, the spy's skin burned. He bit down on the pain, refusing to show his weakness. A chill crept into his bare feet from the dank dungeon water. Seven wardens, two Mooncursed, and several more imperial guards filled the cell.

Sweat beaded on his brow as he gritted his teeth through the waves of pain. The shadows he hadn't known inhabited his body were writhing under his skin. His fingers flickered in and out of existence—fighting against the titan ore chains, but he was trapped.

The cell door slammed open, and Emperor Rexil strode in, followed by his advisor, Eryx. The emperor's gaze roved over the spy as if memorizing every small detail.

The emperor stopped two paces away. "I don't recognize your face. I've poured over the night my map burned. I meditated on every detail of you and yet... you are not known to me."

Emperor Rexil circled the chair, and the spy forced his gaze straight.

"I'd almost wonder if it was you," the emperor continued. "But your eyes tell me we've met. Many times. I wonder how often I walked past you not realizing. How many times your fingers twitched for a blade."

The nameless one kept his expression masked. Things were only about to get worse. He had to remain focused to endure.

"Do you wish you'd have killed me? Do you wish you'd taken the chance?"

Let go. Go somewhere else.

"Who are you working for?" the emperor pressed.

Don't react.

The emperor continued circling. "Who sent you? What are your plans?"

Don't react.

The spy stared forward, trying to appear bored. This was a mid-week luncheon, and he was merely annoyed by a nosy neighbor. He wasn't about to be tortured.

"What is your name?"

Don't react.

His lip curled anyways.

The emperor paused. "Your name? It matters to you for some reason?" The emperor leaned close enough that the spy could smell lotus flowers and copper. "Then I'm going to take it from you, just like you took my map from me."

The spy stared forward, angry at himself for giving anything away, refusing to meet the emperor's gaze.

"I'm going to break you, and then you'll give me everything."

The spy's gaze finally dragged toward the emperor, as if his skin wasn't already crawling with titan ore chains that felt like fire ants.

"We'll see," he replied.

Emperor Rexil released him. "Eryx, bring the spike."

The spy resumed glaring at the damp stones and gleaming shadows dancing in the far corner. If he could only get free of these chains and reach them.

Eryx snapped his fingers, and a warden brought forward a mallet and titan ore spike. The warden passed them to the Emperor. The spy's breath came shallow as instinctual dread roiled his blood.

You can do this. Quiet the mind. Keep breathing and let this world fall away. Fear serves no purpose. Just let go.

The spy's hands shook as adrenaline pumped his veins. No matter how strong the mind, sometimes the body still reacted on its own. The emperor pressed the spike into the fragile bones in the spy's hand.

The chains hurt bad enough. *A spike... gods, it would be terrible.* The spy fought his fear, staring straight ahead and gritting his teeth.

Emperor Rexil smiled mirthlessly. "Are you already afraid?"

"Of course, but only a fool forgets the gods will judge him in death."

The emperor's gaze narrowed. "I do the will of my goddess."

"We'll see what Dhagaos, the god of death, has to say about that. We'll see how X'era reacts."

Without warning, the emperor hammered the spike through the spy's hand. The spy shouted in agony, writhing against the foreign magic invading his bones. Blood dripped from the spy's mouth as shadows ravaged his body to escape the titan ore until he was left shuddering.

The emperor knelt, inspecting the hand and black veins darkening the flesh. "You have some sort of magic. It's why it took us so long to find you."

"Or you're really bad at finding people." The spy coughed blood onto the floor.

The emperor tapped the mallet against the spy's bare foot. "You won't be so stealthy with a limp. Tell me your name."

The nameless one said nothing.

Crunch.

The mallet came down atop the arch of his foot. His hips lifted from the chair as blinding pain wracked his body. His eyes searched wildly for a shadow to escape through, but the titan ore anchored him.

"I'll kill you!" the spy bellowed.

"You could try, but Niamh protects me." The emperor pressed his fist against the bone shards floating inside his foot, each sending blinding pinpricks of pain into the spy's skull. "What's your name?"

"Rot in the worst of the hells," the spy spat.

"I wonder what could have caused you to betray your people so thoroughly."

The spy, shaking, replied, "My grandfather found his wife's broken body and dug his son out of the burning rubble of his home from all the pointless fighting. The conquering. The greed. The hate."

The emperor tilted his head. "That's exactly what I seek to end—the fighting. I united the continent, conquering everyone so there would be no more fighting."

"And yet your people starve. Disappear. Monsters roam your streets."

Gods—the spike hurt so badly.

He was already fighting not to lose his nerve.

Emperor Rexil threw up his hands. "If I wasn't focusing on dealing with pointless resistance, I could build. You could have been fighting for us with me, instead of against me."

"Your cost of peace is too high. Niamh's cost is too high."

The spy would black out soon. The spike in his hand clashed with his shadow magic, and his organs were crushed between the two.

Doubt darkened the emperor's eyes, but he said, "She will crush the resistance and save us all."

"It is she we need saving from," the spy said weakly.

Eryx handed the emperor a curved, paper-thin blade. A skinning knife. The spy blinked back uncontrolled tears.

Godsdamn him.

The emperor nodded and a warden ripped the spy's pants open at the knee. The emperor knelt, the knife hovering above the spy's thigh.

"Your name?"

The spy tried to clear his mind and flee to a pearly lake with floating lotus flowers under an indigo sky. Just as he'd been trained. It wasn't so easy as that. As the knife slipped under his skin, he started screaming. The Mooncurseds' ears laid flat, and the guards looked away.

"You won't destroy all I've built," the emperor said coldly. "All I've sacrificed for. Tell me your plans. Tell me your name."

The pain was unbearable. The cool air was sharp against his raw flesh. His shattered foot swelled with blood. His hand still burned, and his organs felt bruised. The nameless one's mind began shutting down to protect him.

The spy looked up. "No."

He fought to let go, to escape this world, at least in his mind.

"I'm going to take your name from you," Emperor Rexil said.

The screaming went on for hours.

Huddled in a ball in the center of the cell, the spy tried to move as little as possible. He tried to stop existing. Bandages covered the stubs of his missing fingers and the strip of skin carved from his leg. They wanted him in agony, but they didn't want him to die just yet. Yet, death was all he prayed for. In X'era's mercy, he'd be gone soon.

His foot was barely tingling—a bad sign. His hand quivered from the titan ore spike. They'd removed the chains when they finally left, and he'd tried to shadowstep but the spike anchored him. The magic wouldn't let him remove it. He'd tried until the hand was a swollen, gnarled mess.

Hopeless, he huddled, waiting for the next session. He'd bought Avyllon as much time as possible and sent letters to Aurienne with all he knew. He could die knowing he'd done all he could, and he'd kept his promises.

The cell door swung open, and he immediately started shaking at the thought of what would come.

"Are you ready to talk?" the emperor asked.

He squeezed his eyes shut.

"I'm sorry to hear that," the emperor said.

He actually sounded sorry.

Eryx yanked on the chain and dragged the spy to the chair, hauling him up by the spike. Then Eryx's fist exploded against the spy's cheek, cracking the bones in his face. Fists hammered the spy's ribs and stomach, until the spy vomited. Then Eryx selected a club. The wood cracked against the spy's bones until his head lolled as each strike sapped his strength.

In his mind, he waded through a golden pond with floating stars. It had been difficult at first to find these quiet moments, but it grew easier as his body weakened. His mind must know fighting was pointless, and the end came soon.

Reality came crashing back as a titan ore chain looped around his neck and pulled his head back. The emperor watched as Eryx positioned a long titan ore needle over the spy's open eye.

"What is your name?"

"No!" the spy screamed.

He writhed and twisted, the titan ore choking him as he struggled. Eryx stabbed the needle down, digging around in the spy's eye until it burst. Half his world went dark as his skull throbbed. He thrashed against the chains, screaming until his voice failed him.

X'era!

"What is your name? Who are you working for?" The same questions repeated over and over until he disassociated with reality.

A hot iron pressed against his shoulder, dragging him away from his peaceful lakes.

"What is your name?"

The iron sizzled against his flesh again.

His name floated on his lips, ready to slip out to end the pain. He pushed the name down, down, into the memories he'd forgotten he had. Below the colors of the flowers in his mother's garden. Below the last time he'd seen his father. Down, down, past all the precious things.

The crack of a whip nearly brought him back.

"What is your name?"

"No!" the spy screamed.

He wrapped the name in all the forgotten things. All the secrets he'd nearly wiped from his memory. He stuffed it so far away he couldn't even remember.

"What is your name?"

His body shook violently against the pain of the rodents they'd brought biting him, supping on the blood. The screams stopped long ago as his throat was too raw to make any sound. Snot and tears mixed on his face. The room stank of blood and loose bowels.

"What is your name?"

Eryx cut him, removing appendages, and he fought his own fear and pain. From the moment Mei betrayed him and he decided not to run, death was the only release. He just had to keep his secrets until X'era claimed him for Dhagaos.

"What is your name?"

Eryx grabbed his neck, forcing him to look at him. The spy continued to hide his name under every cut, every second of pain he endured. Fighting for survival, his brain took his secrets and sank them into a dark hole of his mind. And it locked the door for good.

"I have no name. And your soul will burn in the worst of the hells," the spy whispered.

Eryx shoved him to the ground and dragged the chair from the cell. The emperor left without a word. Days passed that felt like years, the torture melding together.

The spy curled into a ball. He couldn't feel his broken foot at all now and his brow beaded with feverish sweat. His leg burned, the rot from the dingy cell setting in. If he survived—he'd lose the foot and the leg most likely. He pressed his hand with the missing fingers against his ruptured eye. There'd be no healing it either.

Nor any of the other injuries.

Slowly, they were breaking his body, and as they did, his brain fled reality. His body shook as his mind fought to shut off the pain. Faraway, he stood on the mountains of Nyx'ela, the realm of the gods. His memories bled away as grains of sand in an hourglass. There was no more pain.

Not much longer now.

NAMELESS
CHAPTER SEVENTEEN

Body failing, the spy was nearly too weak to move. His torturers hadn't realized the effect titan ore would have on his body, didn't know the magical battlefield littering his bones. They'd been careful to keep him alive these past days, but their efforts would soon fall short.

He couldn't move his burning leg at all, and his foot had long lost any feeling. His fingers and eye were gone. All his limbs were flickering, fighting the titan ore. Blood trickled from his lips in a steady dribble.

Gleaming, inky shadows caught his attention. He could almost see the shadow world and worlds beyond. He could almost see X'era's divine face peering back at him but just out of reach. His body was failing.

I wish I could help Avyllon. I wish I could free Demorra. I let the hate of my grandfather close my eyes to the needs of my homeland, but the emperor was right about one thing. I could have been fighting for Demorra. I should have been. It's too late now.

He closed his eyes and drifted away again. His feet crunched on fallen petals as he walked through a forest of blooming tiger lilies. He stopped on a ruby the size of a mountain overlooking silver waves. The silver mist sprayed his face and stuck to his skin like tree sap. The moon loomed closer and closer, casting a long shadow across the continent. Wolf howls cut the air. Letters wrapped in red twine rained from gilded clouds. Aurienne's secret message popped into his brain.

This world makes monsters of us all.

Forcing his eyes open, he looked longingly at the shadows in the cell. Maybe he didn't need his body. He'd nearly become a shadow once before. The way the shadows inside him reacted to the titan ore told him that he'd changed to the core. Could he became a shadow?

Hadn't X'era said something similar?

Beware, little shade. If you stray too long in the shadows, your body will turn to smoke, and your soul will be all that remains.

He'd been fighting losing himself this whole time, but maybe losing himself was exactly what could save him. He could shed his body and let his soul fly free. He could become a monster, and monsters would win this war.

To destroy a monster, you had to become a monster.

This entire time, he had the answer, he'd just been blind to it. He was born for the shadows. This world would no longer be his home, but it hadn't ever been. He'd become a creature of shadows drifting between worlds, no longer tethered to this one.

It was time to let go.

Weakly, he called out, "Summon the emperor, I'm ready to talk."

Was it his imagination, or were the shadows growing, stretching across the cell—reaching for him, welcoming him home. They knew he'd join them as he always was going to.

He detached his mind from his body. Shutting off the pain, he stilled. His heart slowed as he willed himself to be unseen, willed himself to be invisible. He reached for every memory where he'd lived in the shadows and wrapped his mind with them. A chill settled on his burning skin as the sound trickled away like it always did. Being this close to death finally opened the full breadth of his magic to him.

The shadows in his body fought against the titan ore—and he faded from body to smoke. If he stepped into the shadow now, he'd lose his body forever, but it was broken beyond healing anyways. Time to become what he'd always been meant to.

A dark pool at his feet turned inky, gleaming in the torchlight. He smiled.

There you are.

Biting down on a scream, he pulled himself to stand on his non-broken foot. His back was hunched and bowed from the beatings, but he stood as straight as he could manage. He tore X'era's invisible ring from his finger—for he would no longer need to be bound to this world or its shadowy sister. Not once he lost his corporeal form forever. The ring bounced off the stone once and then disappeared into the worlds beyond the veil.

The cell door opened, and the spy dimly turned toward the emperor.

"Are you ready to give me what I want?" the emperor said.

The puddle at the nameless one's feet buzzed with a song only he could hear, one meant for him. "You wanted my name? I'll tell you my secret."

The spy took a step forward, toes brushing the edge of the puddle. Vaguely, he realized he didn't remember his name anymore.

"The secret?" The spy's body was flickering wildly as he spoke.

The emperor's expression changed, as if realizing something was wrong. "Guards!"

"Shadows don't have names."

The nameless one stepped into the inky shadow on a moonless night and became a shade. The shackles clinked to the floor in the dungeon cell as the nameless one vanished.

THE SHADOW'S CITY
CHAPTER EIGHTEEN

His body fought for precious moments in the shadow world, but then it faded away. The nameless one's soul detached forever. All the worlds connected, touching where the veils met. He could see it now. All the roads between the realms. Between the heavens and the hells.

Beams of light and darkness, like threads of a tapestry, spanned space and time to connect the realms. He watched golden souls floating from this world to the place they called the hells—to the afterlife. Shared clouds and oceans linked them. Fish and birds traveled the worlds and back. Rainbows of colors he'd never seen before lit the skies. He could travel forever and not even see everything.

And the *magic*.

In his shadow vision, magic was pure glowing sunlight mixed with crackling lightning and glimmering starlight. Every world's magic was so different, and yet the same.

The magic of *this* world was raging. The ancient, deeply embedded magic writhed against a darkness spreading through the roots of the world. It glowed brighter than all the worlds around it. Angrily, it sparked and cracked, dwarfing the rest. The darkness infecting this world could be traced to another dead one that had crashed into it.

The two worlds warred with magic. It threatened to destroy them both.

The shade looked beyond. The others were so beautiful and vibrant. Nothing anchored him to this world anymore. He could leave and go anywhere.

But first... he'd made a promise.

He turned his attention to this world and slipped back inside. When he stepped out of the shadow, he was smoke. His body, dead and gone, didn't follow this time. He touched the side of a building. Amorphous, his fingers slipped right through.

The nameless one went first to Niamh's temple, but he could not break in. Even walking between all the worlds—it was warded with magic he could not break. He then went to the imperial palace. As before, it was warded. He flitted by the pyramid, sensing weakened wards there as well.

Assassination attempts appeared out of the question. He'd have to rely on Avyllon to help him destroy the emperor. Perhaps, the High Seer would have a vision on how to defeat him and his goddess.

Until then, he had one goal now: to weaken Niamh. They needed prisoners to grow the Mooncursed army, so he'd start there. He started to walk but stopped. If he couldn't touch the world anymore, gravity shouldn't constrain him.

Willing himself to be weightless, he floated into the air. Anything was possible now. His mind was his only barrier.

The nameless one flew faster than he'd ever run. Faster than anyone had ever run. He arrived at the sprawling public city prisons and slipped through the walls. He floated, invisible, in a long hallway of cells.

He willed himself to be seen, a swirling shadow pushed into the shape of the man he'd once been.

Gasps.

Cries.

Feet shuffling away.

"Look!" someone hissed.

Prisoners woke, rousing others to point at him. The prisoners stared at him like a devil. They held their breath, shaking, but didn't even scream.

Guo pushed to the front of the crowd. The imperial guards had somehow found him as well. Jun pushed to the front of another cell. The spy grimaced. He should have listened to Jun's warnings.

The spy hovered, searching the room for the cell key.

"Feng?" Jun asked.

"The nameless shade?" Guo asked in disbelief.

"I am the spy who worked with you in the bakery, and whom Mei brought to you. I'm here to free you all," the spy answered. "Where is the key?"

"On the guard," Jun said, face paling.

The spy dove into the shadows, slipping between worlds to find the guard who was returning from the privy. The nameless one willed his shadowy form to take up the entire hall.

The man shouted.

He turned to run the other way, but the spy blocked him with more shadows, and the corridor became an impenetrable wall of darkness with the spy's face pushing through.

"What do you want?" The guard's teeth chattered as he spoke.

"Free the prisoners. All of them," the nameless one said.

"I can't..."

The spy made his voice boom. "Free them or I'll drag you to the worst of all the hells."

It wasn't a bluff. The spy was confident he could figure out how to accomplish it. His clothes went with him through the shadows. He bet he could drag someone with him to fall forever through the worlds.

One day, he would toss Eryx into the worst realm he could find.

"Okay." The man cowered.

The spy parted the shadows like curtains, guiding the man back to the cells. He opened the first cell with shaking hands and stumbled to the second. One of the prisoners moved to strike the guard, but the spy covered the prisoner in shadows.

"We are all victims here. Leave in peace," the spy said.

The attacker backed away, pale as the moonlight, nodding.

Cell after cell opened and the prisoners fled into the night. The keys rattled in the guard's hand as the last prisoner slipped away.

"You'd be better off joining the rebellion," the spy observed.

Then he was gone.

Floating through the city, his eyes adjusted to his new form. He noticed strands of magic going on forever in every direction. And then he noticed the bowls.

A faint, purple, pulsing light connected the offering bowls back to the main temple. Each one connected to the next in a giant spiderweb to Niamh's temple. He descended to the closest bowl, filled with notes and coins and ribbons. He reached for it, but his hand went through the offerings.

Growling, he realized he couldn't interact with it.

The bowls were feeding Niamh power. If he could destroy them, he could weaken her.

A dark object appeared and rolled against his foot. He felt it. Eyes widening, he bent down to pick it up.

X'era's ring.

It melted into a puddle in his hand, swirling like a living thing. He glanced at the crystal bowl. If only he had something to break it with. The ring-puddle exploded, taking the shape of a long black staff.

The spy tapped the bottom of the staff against the bowl. It clinked. Reaching back, he swung the staff at it. As it broke, purple light exploded like lightning. The light in the nearby house turned on, and people came out. The spy floated to the next and cracked it.

One by one, bowls exploded, and the light burned out. Gritting his teeth, he swung the staff again and again. Purple pottery went flying in every direction. Purple light flared. The web of power dimmed.

An ethereal scream pierced the night from Niamh's temples. He shattered the containers, flitting through the city like a wraith circling inward in a spiral of destruction. People gathered to watch the purple lightning streaking outward from the broken pottery. He'd gotten a third of them broken before the air changed.

Newly taken souls flew toward the afterlife.

A massive sacrifice.

Niamh had noticed him, and she was angry.

A rageful, searching presence slithered through the city, sealing doorways and seeking him out. It was destructive and snuffing and oily, and he sensed that if it caught him, it'd devour his soul. He couldn't stay here any longer in the seat of her power. He'd done what he could, but it was time to leave.

His eyes drifted toward the shrine—a nightmarish monument to the evil rooted in this city. He couldn't free the Mooncursed or stop the priestesses from their dark magic. There were too many, and he didn't have enough time before Niamh expelled him from of the city. There was only one mercy he could offer those poor souls.

Chaos.

Haunting Melody
Chapter Nineteen

The pyramid illuminated the sleeping city with gutters of burning oil. The nameless one drifted across the ridges of the pyramid, walking where no one had for centuries.

X'era—give me the strength for this one mercy.

The weakened wards flickered, exposing a hole in their protections.

Thank you.

Feeling his magic flare as his death fueled it, he followed the oil channels inside the pyramid, stepping through walls and gliding unnoticed past Mooncursed.

He found the vats quickly. Barrels of oil as tall as two-level buildings made from ancient trees. Perfect for what he planned. His ring warmed on his hand. It had worked to destroy the bowls. Maybe it would work for this too.

He willed the ring to become the staff again, and it snapped open in his hand. He pressed the staff against the barrel until a small trickle of oil seeped out. It seemed that there was more to X'era's gift than he realized. He traced the oil into a stream leading away from the barrels.

Almost feeling the stone beneath his feet again, he strode slowly through the maze—leading the trail of oil. He closed the loop on the outer maze.

A Mooncursed approached, sniffing the air and glaring at him with yellow eyes. The beast was bent in half under the ceilings that had been well over the spy's head. The claws on its paws were as long as a man's arm. It was one of the biggest he'd seen. Its mouth was carved across its face by a blade and rows of fangs peeked out. A growl rumbled in its throat.

The nameless one did not fear it now.

What is already dead can't be killed again.

Now truly looking, he saw details he'd never noticed before on any of them. Its limp, furry tail dragged along the floor, and it reeked of blood and old meat. Deep crisscrossed scars covered its body. Its limbs were gnarled and knobby, as if they'd been broken and healed time and time again.

You're all victims, too.

He paused, looking into the Mooncursed's glowering stare. The glowing yellow eyes were tinged with purple, now that he got this close. And under the bloodthirsty urges was pain.

The nameless one's heart twinged. He knew their pain. The constant torture of being trapped in a body you had no control over. Except his torture lasted days. Theirs had lasted months or longer. All he wanted in those final moments was to be released. It was all he could offer them now.

"I'm going to free you all, the best I can. You won't feel pain anymore," the nameless one said.

He pressed his hand against the beast's head. He couldn't feel it, couldn't really touch it, but he willed understanding through the magic connecting the realms. Hoping the beast would understand. Recalling the memories of his own torture, of Avyllon, of peace, he showed them to the Mooncursed monster.

The Mooncursed's expression dimmed. It turned its head so the nameless one could see the titan ore collar, its barbed prongs digging deeply into its flesh. Black blood oozed out of the collar.

The nameless one pressed the end of his great staff against the collar. Now that he was in his true form, the full magic of the ring burst to life. The collar popped open, as it was no match for X'era's gift. The warden's control vanished. Still a raging, bloodthirsty beast, perhaps it could momentarily direct its rage at its captors. The spy knew he could never release these things into the world, but perhaps he could end their torment.

"I'll help the others either way," the nameless one whispered.

He'd freed it from the magic negating collar. Now, it was up to the beast what it would do. It could sound the alarm. It could run off into the night. He wouldn't blame it for either. But just maybe it would help him.

The Mooncursed threw back its head and howled, long and mournful. The cries echoed through the pyramid's maze. Then it darted toward the inner chamber with the cages.

It's going to help.

Even a beast knew better than to run toward danger unless it was protecting its kin. It knew what it was sacrificing, and yet it led the way. The spy knew that this single moment of clarity wouldn't save the beast. He'd given it a temporary gift, but if it got out into the city—it'd be a massacre.

I still have to do what I came here to do.

The spy finished drawing the lines of oil through the maze, more and more splashing the floors.

The screams tore through the inner chamber. The nameless one slipped into the chamber as the enormous Mooncursed attacked the wardens. They slashed at it with titan ore swords, and it howled in pain at every cut. But it did not stop.

The spy used his staff to pop off the collars, and then he opened the cages. The Mooncursed rushed out, descending on their jailers. The priestesses screamed as they were ripped to pieces.

The spy dragged the oil into a slick circle around the altar. He paused near one of the torches, watching the Mooncursed take their revenge on the wardens and priestesses. Blood sprayed the walls and the floors. Mooncursed died alongside their wardens, locked in lethal battle. The beasts were victims to the real monsters and now sought vengeance.

Over the din, the nameless one locked eyes with the enormous

Mooncursed. The Mooncursed held his gaze as people died all around them. Then it looked away.

The nameless one stifled a sob and knocked the torch off the wall with his staff. It hit the oil and the trail flared. Blazing fires licked the walls, burning the tools with the flesh. Inky tears flowed down his face.

This is a mercy. And it's the evilest thing I've ever seen.

Mooncursed railed against their cages as they burned. Wardens cooked inside their armor. The freed beasts tried to run. The spy backed out of the room as even the mortar between the stones melted. Stone blocks fell, crushing burning cages and the victims within.

A priestess, covered in flames, ran screaming across the chamber before a Mooncursed swiped her with its claws. The air filled with burnt hair and flesh.

And then the oil barrels ignited. Explosions rocked the pyramid. Stones crumbled. The screaming never stopped as the occupants were cooked alive.

The nameless one floated into the sky, watching the pyramid burn. The wretched workshop inside was destroyed. Most of the Mooncursed army was gone. They'd rebuild eventually, but it would take time. Time that Avyllon could use to overthrow the emperor.

Death howls filled the air. Lights in the city turned on as the grating, mournful sound woke the city that was not already awake from the destruction of the offering bowls. The howls of those burning alive were the most tragic sound the nameless one had ever heard.

Each one broke his heart into smaller and smaller pieces. Long after the howls stopped, he could still hear them echoing in his mind. A melody he'd carry with him forever.

"I'm sorry. I did what I could for you," he murmured.

Soul after soul raced into the afterlife. The Mooncursed were now free of the unending pain and torment. The wardens, though, their souls were ripped apart by those they tormented. Those who managed to reach the death god, Dhagaos, were subjected to a far worse fate. He could see it all in those spaces where the realm of the living and the dead collided.

The Mooncursed spirits, now the people they once were, watched him from between the veils of the worlds. He wasn't sure if they were grateful or angry. Sad or confused. Whether they would thank or attack him.

"I will avenge every one of you. And I will help your loved ones. I swear it," he vowed.

The spirits departed, leaving him to his dark work as the phantom howls echoed.

FREE

CHAPTER TWENTY

Alone, Mei lingered atop the city walls overlooking the golden road that stretched to every end of the continent. The spy watched her, gathering the strength he'd need to say goodbye. He sensed Niamh's power growing, the wards tightening and brightening. They'd soon push him out for good.

Tears dripped down Mei's chin as wind whipped the hem of her gray mottled cloak. Her eyes were red and puffy, and she clutched her curved dagger to her chest.

The shadow appeared beside her, sitting on the edge of the wall overlooking the deadly drop, unafraid.

He said, "Spies don't cry."

She jumped and spun, pointing her dagger at him. He stepped forward, allowing the dagger to pass through his formless body. His features flickered in and out of view, sometimes a picture of who he used to be. More often, he was no more than a swirling wraith, a collection of shadows forming the outline of a man.

"It's you?" she asked, eyes widening.

"Yes," he said.

"But how?" she breathed.

"The night we burned the map I fell between worlds. The goddess

X'era found me and saved me. Ever since, I had the ability to shadow-step. The more I did it, the more I lost myself. My body. Time. Finally, I gave it up completely to escape the emperor."

It was her fault. After trusting her when he'd never trusted anyone, she'd betrayed him. He knew she had no choice. He knew she'd have done anything else. And he even knew she was drowning under the guilt. But it didn't change the sting he felt when he remembered her face as the guards dragged him away to be tortured.

The cut was so fresh. So deep. He couldn't blame her, but he couldn't trust her either. There was no use saying any of these things.

She knew.

"I sense they kept their promise to heal you."

Mei sank to the ground. "I'm so sorry. I've been searching for you. Trying to find a way to free you. I'm sorry. Know that I will carry this burden for the rest of my life. Did they..."

"Yes," he replied. "It was worse than I'd imagined. You would do well to avoid getting caught. They ensure that death is the only escape. I lost much of who I was. I forgot my name if you'd believe it."

Tears spilled down her cheeks. "I'm so sorry."

"Don't be." He wanted to reach out and touch her face, but his fingers would slip right through. "You didn't have a choice, and if you could go back in time, you'd have to do it all over again. It's a risk we all take as spies. We know that death awaits. The only question is how you die. I died with my honor and my name."

Mei lifted her chin. "I want to become nameless."

She dropped the hood from her head, revealing that her hair had been chopped to her ears and bleached white. Her expression was now the same as his had been—utterly forgettable. And with a quick twist of the wrist, her hair was black, and face smudged with ash. The cloak was gone, replaced by a laundress's uniform. She twirled and the uniform was replaced with a noble woman's gown, face clean and hair back to white. In a flash, her cloak appeared again.

She said quietly, "From this moment on, I shall no longer have a name. Mei is dead. I am a nameless one."

Pride filled him, along with regret, and feelings of betrayal that he couldn't shake no matter what.

"Teach me to shadowstep. Pull me through the world between worlds," she said. "I want this power."

Before when she'd asked, he hadn't known what to do or how to teach it. Now he did, and he couldn't stand the thought of her forsaking everything. Not yet.

"Perhaps, one day, when there is no other choice, I will show you," he said. "I was a spy for a long time, and there is much that can be done as a nameless one. Before you give away your ability to feel human touch, to love, to have a family—try everything else first."

She paled, still clutching the dagger against her middle. "Oh."

"If you ever ask me again, I will explain it to you. I hope you don't. Once the transformation begins, there is no stopping it. It will overtake you. It is not magic you can dabble in. One shadowstep, and eventually it'll devour you."

He gazed over Rexila's towering temples, reaching spires, and menacing pyramids. Blinking lights from hundreds of thousands of homes fought for survival under the heavy cloud of a tyrant. The golden road stretched across the conquered continent, begging, railing for freedom.

"Are you... going to help us?" she asked quietly.

"Yes." His voice was smooth as oil on polished glass. "But I can't help from here. Not now that Niamh searches for me and wards the entire city. Only Avyllon's High Seer has the power to defeat the emperor and his false goddess. There is nothing else I can do here."

Tears slipped down her face. "Will I see you again?"

He hoped so, one day when the betrayal hurt less. When he might trust her, and she'd discovered the costs of this life. Maybe they'd have missions and adventures together. They'd laugh and joke as easily as breathing. That day wasn't today and might never come. Even if he could stay, even if there was work to be done here, he wouldn't have worked with her. Not yet.

"Only X'era knows," he said.

I trusted you and you betrayed me, and nothing will be the same.

The unspoken words lingered between them.

I'm sorry.

I know.

"Don't stop fighting. Demorra needs you, nameless one," he said. "I hope we meet again."

There would be no hug, no handshake, no kiss on the cheek. No point to the long goodbyes. She was grieving her choice, and he was hurting from it. And there was work to be done. He floated down the wall, away from his once-partner. It was strange to miss someone other than his mother. Leaving other missions, he'd missed places. Never people.

This is what it feels like to have something to lose.

"I'll fight 'til Demorra is free or until I'm dead," she said to the skies. "And I will ask you to teach me shadowstepping. I don't care what it costs." Her expression mirrored titan ore—cold, hard, with bright glints, though hers were furious.

His response was a whisper on the wind. "If you ask, I won't deny you."

The nameless one drifted away from her and lingered in the dark skies, saying farewell to his homeland.

He'd once thought he had no reason to save them, but his grandfather had been wrong. Maybe they weren't worth saving fifty years ago, but they were now. They were ready to try for better. To do better. And they needed his help.

"I'm going to save you," he whispered to all Demorra.

Distant, phantom howls replied.

His father and grandfather had always warned him to never step into a shadow atop dark, still water when the moon was gone, or he might lose his soul. It was that exact misstep that might have been what *saved* his soul by giving him purpose. He would help defeat the emperor and his cruel goddess for the rest of the world. He'd defeat the Mooncursed. Monsters would win this war, and now he'd become one of them.

"You can't defeat a shadow," he whispered.

Nothing more than a nameless shade, he stepped into a shadow and vanished, vowing to one day exact his revenge.

EPILOGUE

Emperor Jhames Rexil knelt in the dungeons with his palm against the dank, stone floor. The spy had been right there, and then simply gone. He'd been over it again and again, replaying those last moments, and there was no trick. Some magic allowed the unnamed one to slip through his fingers, and when he thought he'd been so close to breaking the man.

Jhames grimaced.

He took no pleasure in the crushing of a spirit, the breaking of the body. These distasteful acts were necessary for him to achieve the great purpose laid out for him. If the spy had just given him the information, he wouldn't have had to do any of it. Wistful thinking, he knew. Nothing worth achieving would come easy, but he was determined to push through every obstacle, every resistance.

The scars on the back of his hand were a reminder of why he had to do this. Growing up in one of the war-torn tribes, he'd been raised in bloodshed and savagery with parents gone far too soon.

Jhames remembered the nights he'd spent crying as a young boy, gnawing on frozen roots to mollify his hunger pangs. He could still feel the sting of training blades and punishing whips upon his flesh. The sight of his lost comrades, the maimed innocents, the burned villages never left him. Every night, he dreamed of a land of peace without the fighting or the greed.

The godsdamned raids and pointless fighting that never accomplished anything brought cruelty, waste, and pain. Now, he had the power to put an end to it forever. He'd made a deal with Niamh. She'd give him the magic and power to achieve lasting peace, and he'd help her return to this realm fully. The cost was great, but the reward was far greater. So far, she'd kept up her end of their bargain, so he had to keep his.

Nothing—not the seer or elf, not their growing company of monsters, not even this shadow-walking spy would stand in his way.

Afterword

Thank you for reading!

If you enjoyed *The Nameless Shadow,* please consider leaving a review on Goodreads or Amazon. Reviews, ratings, and word of mouth are so important for independent authors. Every review helps. If you haven't yet read the main series, check out *The High Seer.*

For more information about upcoming works and updates, visit my website www.alexbreewrites.com or follow me on Instagram @alex.bree.writes.

Want to stay up to date? Sign up for my author newsletter for exclusive updates, sneak peeks, and release news.

Alex Bree is a fantasy author and attorney living in Meridian, Idaho, with her husband, children, and dogs.

ACKNOWLEDGMENTS

I am so happy to share with you all this new character, new magic, and a peek into the villainous, conquering empire.

Thank you to my husband Korey who has been my ultimate supporter, first alpha reader, and brainstorm partner. You listen to all my insane musings, first drafts, editing and revising woes, bad poetry attempts, and you never question when the writing process gets weird (and it does). To my children, who inspire me every day, I love you!

Thank you to my writing group partners. I'm so thankful to have found you! You're the first ones I go to when I'm deciding on the million things that go into a book—artwork, artists, editors, blurbs, chapter titles, website design, social media posts, fonts, formatting, obscure grammar questions, and everything else. Thank you: AJ Braun, Billie Grey, Loren Huxley, Jaci M. Lunera, Tiffany O'Haro, PC Nottingham, N.C. Scrimgeour, Nico Vincenty, and Kaela Woodruff.

Special thanks also go to my wonderful friends who have encouraged and supported me: Taylor, Jaime, and Ruth.

Finally, to all those of you who read and enjoyed this book—I want to thank *you*.